Tanner's Promise

Tanner's Promise

A Harlow Brother Romance

Kaylie Newell

TULE
PUBLISHING

Prologue

THE SETTING SUN lit the Montana sky in a slow bleed of fluid purples and burnt oranges the likes of which Tanner Harlow hadn't seen since he was a kid. At least not that he'd noticed since he was a kid. He'd always loved sunsets, though. The ending of days. It was the endings that had given him some peace growing up.

"It was fast, that's a comfort," his aunt Vivian said on the other end of the line. Her voice was monotone, emotionless. It wasn't that there weren't feelings deep down, but this was how she operated in moments like these. No fuss, no muss.

"Yeah," he said, staring out his living room window. Charlotte, his Doberman mix, licked his hand while he rubbed her soft, floppy ears. "It was fast."

There was a pause, and he heard a deep exhale of air. He knew what was coming and he braced himself for it. His heart slowed to a dull thump inside his chest. *Maddie...*

"It only makes sense that she comes to live with us, Tanner," she said. "You know that."

Did he? That was the thing. He really didn't. But now wasn't the time to argue. Now was the time to nod and agree for the sake of getting through this shitty night. His mother had been dead for twelve hours. And he was finding that twelve hours was all it took to turn everything you thought you knew about your life on its head.

He blinked, watching the sun sink toward Copper Mountain's blue-violet hulk in the distance. "Yeah," he said.

"She can stay with you in Marietta for the summer. That'll give us time to get things in order, then I can come out and pick her up. Have you talked to Judd and Luke?"

His brothers were just as shell-shocked as he was. They'd both called—Judd from his layover in Boston, and Luke from where he was stationed in Afghanistan. There was no rule book for a sudden death in a family, no preset conversation that was supposed to take place. But they were on their way. It would be quick—long enough to bury Jennifer Harlow and put their arms around their eleven-year-old half sister, Maddie. Then it was up to Tanner to hold it together until Vivian could take her back to Hawaii in the fall. That was the plan, at least.

Tanner ran his hand over Charlotte's pointy head and the dog closed her eyes in simple canine content. She sat with a soft groan at his feet, maybe sensing he needed the comfort.

"I talked to them," Tanner said. "Judd will be here tomorrow. Luke, Tuesday."

"I got the first flight out of Honolulu in the morning. We'll take care of everything when I get there, okay?"

And what would that look like? Cleaning up the residual mess of his mother's turbulent existence? Making plans to usher Maddie into another state, another life, where he and his brothers would most likely see her only on Christmas if they were lucky?

But what choice did he have? He was twenty-six years old. He'd just started his landscape design business and it was fledgling at best. He'd just taken out a loan, and he needed time to devote to his work or he was going to retire a damn gardener. Which was exactly what his aunt thought he was. Nothing more, nothing less.

Luke and Judd's positions weren't much better. Judd flew constantly and barely had a home base. Luke was in the middle of fighting a war, for God's sake. Which left Tanner. The baby of his brothers. The one who'd stuttered until he was fifteen years old and had barely spoken a word to anyone for two years after that. He was going to be the temporary guardian of his little sister. A temporary *father*. At least until September.

He swallowed the ache in his throat. His mom hadn't been a great parent. She hadn't even been passable for a good part of his life. But she'd been the only one he'd ever known, aside from a father he'd just as soon forget. And he missed her. He missed her at that moment more than she probably deserved.

"Okay, Vivian," he said into the phone. Charlotte pricked her ears at the sound of his voice and he looked down at her. His best friend. A dog. But Tanner Harlow wasn't in the business of trusting most anyone on two legs. That was just the dirty truth of the matter. "Have a safe flight."

Chapter One

F RANCIE TATE LISTENED to the guy talking at her from a
few feet away. And that was an accurate description.
Talking *at* her, instead of talking *to* her. Specifically, he was
having a conversation with her boobs.

Aware that her cleavage swelled over the neck of her
white tank top, she crossed her arms over her chest and took
a step back.

"You're just gonna have to take this here wall down if
you want more room," the guy was saying. He'd taken his
cap off and was using it to fan himself. Sweat beaded along
his minimal hairline, and his face was ruddy as a vine-
ripened tomato. His gaze flickered to her chest and back up
again.

Francie forced a smile, because that's what she did. She
smiled whether she wanted to or not because she was bubbly
and sweet. Everyone said so. She could almost hear her mom
repeating it in her ear, while leaning down to fluff her hot
roller curls. *Now, smile, Francie! Show 'em what a nice girl you
are!*

"I see," she said, looking back at the wall. The room was
cramped, that was true. She was no contractor, but she

didn't see how she would achieve more space without knocking it down, either. However, she wasn't made of money. She loved this little house. She was so proud of the fact that she'd bought it on her own, no help from her parents, and on a teacher's salary, too. That was no easy feat. But it needed work.

Anxiety curled in her lower belly, and she pushed the thought away that maybe she'd bitten off more than she could chew.

She extended her hand. "I'll have to think about it, Bill. Thank you."

He shook it, stepping into her personal space. He was the fourth guy she'd called to come out and take a look at the living room, and she vowed he'd be the last. She didn't like how his eyes, small and set too closely together, kept taking her in like she was a slab of meat.

By now she was used to workers coming in and trying to intimidate her. They never took her seriously. To them she was the clichéd petite blonde. And she went right along with it, because she didn't know how to be anyone else. Even though it made her sick to her stomach. Even though what she really wanted to do was plant her foot right between their legs.

"I don't have to rush off," he said, still grasping her hand. "We haven't talked price yet."

"No, we haven't. But I have a few other people coming over. I'll have to call you."

"Don't call me, I'll call you?"

She felt sweat prickle between her breasts. June in Marietta wasn't the most comfortable without a working window unit, which she didn't have. Plus, the guy had passed inappropriate a few seconds ago and was now working his way into unsettling, with a hefty side of weird. Where in the world had she gotten his name? From anyone reputable? She made a mental note to remember and kill them later.

"Hello?"

There was a sharp knock on the screen door, and Francie felt a rush of relief all the way to her toes.

Bill what's-his-face finally let go and put his cap back on as if he'd been about to do it all along. She wiped her hand on her cutoffs and narrowed her eyes at him.

"One hundred and eight Bramble Lane? Hope I'm not too early."

Francie turned at the sound of the low, male voice. She didn't care who it was. Didn't care if it was the IRS coming to audit her for eternity. She wanted to kiss his feet.

Standing outside the screen door was a tall, broad-shouldered man. Worn, dirty jeans, white T-shirt that was dirty, too. His baseball cap rode low over his eyes, and he leaned against the doorjamb with the casual confidence that only a man who was incredibly tall could pull off without looking too cocky. His dark hair was shaggy and stuck out from underneath the cap, brushing the nape of his neck. Her first thought was *hot. Holy crap, this guy is hot.* Her second was that he looked familiar.

He was looking right past her, though, and directly at the contractor who jingled his keys in his hand.

"I was just leaving," Bill said, avoiding the other man's

gaze. "Let me know if you want a quote, and I'll come back."

"No, thanks," she bit out. Which wasn't like her. Wasn't like her at all. But there was something about the guy on her front porch, and the fact that she wasn't alone anymore that gave her the confidence to be a little bitchy. The words felt liberating on her tongue. She pushed her shoulders back and stepped aside so Bill what's-his-face could pass in a fragrant cloud of sweat and tobacco.

He gave her a funny look, as though he didn't know what in the world he'd done, and brushed out the door without another word.

Francie looked at the guy on her porch again and smiled. *The landscape designer.* Of course. That'd explain the dirty jeans. The deliciously dirty T-shirt that was a loose fit, but it did absolutely nothing to hide the defined chest underneath.

And there it was again—the sense that she knew him from somewhere, but she couldn't figure out where. First of all, nobody she knew was that tall. She'd remember the height alone. It kind of commanded attention. But the way he held himself, that slight tilt to his shoulders, nagged at her subconscious.

She walked over to the screen door, her bare feet padding on the hardwood floor. "Quaking Aspen Landscape?" She remembered the name because it was so pretty. Aspens were her favorite.

The guy nodded, pushing off the doorjamb and putting his hands in his jean pockets. "Sorry. Hope I didn't interrupt anything."

"With that guy?" She laughed. "Yeah, my murder maybe.

Come on in."

She unlatched the door and pushed it open. The late afternoon sunlight slanted warm and golden into her little bungalow, making it hard to see his face.

Shielding her eyes, she breathed deeply the musky scent of man and earth as he passed. Maybe a little soap from earlier in the day. It was more heady than she would've liked. Definitely more heady than she felt comfortable with. She'd sworn off men for a while. She wasn't supposed to be noticing things like tanned forearms and jeans that rode low on narrow hips. Honestly, though, she'd just sworn off assholes. She couldn't remember anything about swearing off super-attractive landscapers who showed up at precisely the right moment, wearing precisely the right clothing to make her ovaries sit up and take notice.

He walked in, the floor creaking under his weight. With his back still turned, she wondered again where she knew him. She hadn't been back in Marietta long enough to have crossed paths with anyone new. She must recognize him from before. Francie wasn't an egomaniac, but she *had* been a self-absorbed teenager with a doting fan base. As an adult, she was used to people in town knowing her, but not being able to place them right away. And that always led to awkward moments like these that made her feel like a complete jerk.

She hooked her thumbs in her back pockets as he took his hat off and turned around. The absence of it left a sexy, athlete-style ring around his hair that she immediately pictured running her hands through.

He was tan. Really tan. There were white crinkles radiating from the corners of his brown eyes, a dark shadow of a beard along his jaw. She was positive now. She definitely knew this guy…

"I was wondering if that was you," he said. He didn't look at her when he said it. He held his hat in both hands, pinching the rim between his thumb and fingers. His gaze, *that gaze,* was averted. The one she recognized as being so shy that it had broken her heart once. *In high school?*

She felt her mouth go slack. She couldn't help it. The memories came rushing back then, in a torrent so powerful, they nearly knocked her over with their vividness.

"Tanner?" she managed. "Tanner Harlow?" But it couldn't be Tanner. Tanner was still a boy. Skinny, with a terrible stutter that made it almost impossible for him to talk at all. He was the kid who'd tugged on her heartstrings in first period English. The kid that her asshat boyfriend, Guy Davis, had picked on relentlessly, no matter how often Francie tried to intervene.

He looked at her then, just as he had all those years ago. Those deep brown eyes. How could she have forgotten them?

"Yeah," he said. "It's me."

She didn't know what to say. How long since she'd seen him last? Eight years, maybe? Nine? And he looked so different. She'd heard of boys having their growth spurts late, but she'd never really seen the result of one until now.

And the stutter was gone. That awful stutter that had tormented him and broken her heart. Tanner Harlow was all grown up and standing here in her living room. And she'd just been staring at his butt, for God's sake.

Cheeks burning, she stepped forward to hug him. "I can't believe it."

He bent and hugged her back, his arm encircling her waist. His body felt just as hard as it looked, and for the first time in a long time, Francie found herself flustered. She didn't usually get flustered. When other people laughed nervously, Francie flipped her hair and smiled. When other people struggled for the right words, Francie had a basketful of them, and then some. It was her schtick.

Stepping back, she beamed up at him. Sweat now crawled at her temples. She fanned herself with her hand and shook her head.

"You look great," she said. "I didn't recognize you. You're so different than…" *Shit, shit, shit.*

His eyes cooled a little.

"I'm sorry," she said, wanting to bite her tongue in half. "I didn't mean—"

"It's okay. No more stutter, right?"

Her pulse quickened. "No. But you've grown up, too."

"So have you."

She touched her hair, pulled back into a messy bun. All of a sudden, she realized how she must look. *Murphy's Law.* Put lip gloss on, and you saw nobody. Go without a shower for two days, and bump into your entire graduating class.

He put his hands in his pockets, his expression unreadable. His jaw muscles were working, though. Clenching and unclenching underneath that stubble.

"It's been a while, Francie," he said. "You've been away from Marietta for…how long now?"

"Since high school. I came back this spring. My dad isn't doing well, so I wanted to be close."

"I'm sorry to hear that."

"It's working out, I missed home. And I'll be teaching third grade in the fall."

He smiled, two long dimples cutting into his cheeks. "You were always good with kids."

"I don't know about that," she said. "But I do love them. What about you? A landscape designer? I'm impressed."

He shrugged, glancing out the window. "I'm lucky. Get to be outside. Get to work with my hands."

Before she could help it, she wondered what else he could do with his hands.

"Do you ever see anyone from high school?" she asked, clearing her throat. Then realized it was a dumb question. She couldn't think of anyone from school Tanner would *want* to see.

"Not a ton. Allison Sanders is still around. Billy Reeves, that group…I see Guy sometimes."

At the sound of the name, she stiffened. There was something in his expression that suggested he might be poking her a little. Seeing what her reaction would be. Guy had been an absolute jackass as a teenager. He was still a jackass, but he had money, and money tended to make people accept the jackiest of asses. She'd seen him around, too. He kept trying to make a coffee date to "catch up," and she kept coming up with lame excuses. Why didn't she just tell him to take a long walk off a short pier?

"Oh, yeah," she said. "I've seen him a few times, too. We're all getting so *old*."

There was the coolness again. The way his eyes hardened just a fraction. She'd brushed the subject of Guy off as tidily as she could manage, just like she always had. And now there was a sizable elephant in the room.

But that was Francie. Polyanna Francie, her brother used to call her, right before rolling his eyes. She guessed if she admitted what a jerk Guy had been, she'd have to admit to dating him, too. Admit to being his girlfriend during all the awful things he'd done. Albeit while her back was turned, but still. She'd finally broken up with him, but it hadn't been soon enough. And Tanner had grown some balls long before she ever had.

As she remembered that, remembered how surprised everyone had been the day Tanner Harlow snapped, her stomach squeezed.

She clasped her hands together and rocked forward on her bare feet. The cottage had grown quiet, with nothing but the sound of the fan whirring from the bedroom down the hall. She'd been working on the trim in there, and the sharp, tangy smell of paint tickled her nose.

"Should I show you the yard?" she asked, her voice an octave too high. He made her nervous. It wasn't just his looks, which would've made any woman nervous. She felt she owed him something. An apology? An explanation? Neither seemed to fit. Maybe it was just plain guilt. She'd made mistakes as a kid. Hadn't been the perfect girl everyone thought she was. Thinking about it now, she clenched her teeth.

"Sure," he said. "Lead the way."

Turning her back to him wasn't easy. She'd kept herself up okay. *Okay*, not great. She went to the gym sometimes, but honestly, she'd rather be eating Oreos. She walked the country roads of Marietta in the spring and summer with her earbuds in, but skipped the walking altogether when the snow came. Which usually came early. And stayed late. And that just about summed up the current state of her derriere, which had been tight as a drum at seventeen. At twenty-six? Not as tight. Not as shapely, either.

She headed to the screen door wondering if he was looking at it, or her bare legs that were smeared with paint. She could've at least shaved them. At least that.

He reached around her and pushed the door open before she could touch it. She turned and smiled, appreciating the bulge of his biceps, and how his dark, olive skin contrasted with the white T-shirt. He'd really grown into a breathtakingly sexy man. And with a quiet, brooding demeanor to match. *Dear Lord.*

"Here we are," she said, stepping out onto the deck. The paint out here was peeling, unashamed of its current plight. In fact, it seemed joyful, and completely determined to fall off by summer's end. The pink roses lining the front yard were beautiful though. As was the heavy, twisting wisteria that was in desperate need of a trellis to hold it properly over the deck. The yard was wild and perfumed with flowers, most of which she didn't know the names. She needed someone to tame it. To define it a little, but keep its original secret garden charm. She had no idea how to do it, since she killed houseplants on the regular.

She looked over at his truck parked in the shade; a big, white Toyota Tundra with the *Quaking Aspen* logo on the side. The windows were down, and a tween girl with glasses was hanging her long, thin arms out over the passenger door. A sleek black dog with funny eyebrows leaned out the back window. They both looked bored.

"Oh!" Francie said. "I didn't realize you weren't alone."

Tanner nodded toward the truck. "That's my little sister, Maddie."

At the mention of her name, the girl smiled, showing a gap between two front teeth that stuck out a little. Her dark blond hair fell in a mop toward one eye, accentuating the awkwardness. Francie's heart squeezed. She loved kids this age. They were all knobby knees and pointy elbows.

She wiggled her fingers at her, and Maddie waved back.

"Would she like to come in for some lemonade?"

"We don't want to trouble you," Tanner said, his voice taking on a definite tone. All business.

"It's no trouble."

Frowning, he glanced at the truck and back again. "Let's see about your yard, okay?"

Maddie, seeming to have read something in his expression, retreated inside the cab and put her head back against the rest. After a second, she pushed her glasses up to rub her eyes.

Was she crying? Francie glanced at Tanner, who was now

kneeling to inspect a sprinkler head, his T-shirt stretching over a well-defined back. He obviously didn't want to address the little girl in the truck, at least not with Francie. She guessed there were plenty of reasons he could be taking his little sister around on jobs with him, but none of them made a whole lot of sense to her teacher brain at the moment. Instinctively, she wanted to butt in. Insist that Maddie come inside for a glass of lemonade, maybe watch some TV for a few minutes. But also instinctively, she kept her mouth shut. Probably wise. Tanner didn't seem to be in any mood to deal with interference.

With one more look at the little girl and the dog, who now had its head on her shoulder, Francie turned to Tanner and tried to focus more on the sprinkler head and less on broad, muscular shoulders.

"Okay," she said. "What's this gonna run me?"

Chapter Two

T ANNER SAT ON one of the stools that was bolted to the floor in front of the sturdy counter at the Main Street Diner. Maddie sat beside him, twisting in her seat and sucking on a vanilla milkshake. He owed her that much. The poor kid had been with him all afternoon and hadn't complained once. Neither had Charlotte. He made a mental note to give the dog a bite of steak the next time he had one.

He felt like a shit. He couldn't keep this up. Couldn't keep dragging her along on these bids, much less on the jobs that would start up in earnest in the next few weeks. Word had gotten around Marietta that he had some talent and worked hard for a paycheck. He'd even gotten a few calls from outside the county that he hadn't had time to return yet. Hadn't had time, because he was trying to juggle a brand-new business and watch over Maddie at the same time. The two mixed like oil and water.

Flo appeared with his buffalo burger, her hair sprayed harder than a brick in its signature beehive updo, and grinned.

"How's the milkshake, hon?" she asked Maddie.

Maddie smiled back with the straw between her teeth

and gave a thumbs-up.

"I'm not losing my touch, then." She set the overflowing plate on the counter and turned her attention to Tanner. "And how are things with you? Getting along okay?"

There was more to the question than met the ears. *How are you doing since your mom passed? How are you managing with this little girl? When are those brothers of yours coming back to help?*

He'd heard them all before from well-meaning people in town.

"Okay. Maddie's settling in. Luke and Judd are working on coming home. Something more permanent. You know." It was his stock answer.

She nodded, her sharp eyes missing nothing. "But how are *you* doing?"

He picked up the burger, melted pepper jack cheese oozing out the sides. "As well as can be expected. Under the circumstances."

She nodded again. "Uh-huh. So Luke and Judd are coming home eventually…"

"As soon as they can."

"And in the meantime, you're taking this little angel to work with you?"

He took a bite. Big enough that he wouldn't have to answer right away. Someone walked by and slapped him on the back.

"Hey, man. Don't forget to chew."

He looked over his shoulder to see his physical therapist, EJ Corpa, walking out the door. He had a running appointment with him, since lifting seventy-five-pound bags of rock wasn't exactly great on his knee. Tanner nodded in response, cheeks bulging.

Flo stood there and watched, maddeningly patient.

Finally, he did swallow, then took a swig of foamy beer to wash it down. "Yes, Flo. For the time being." He wiped his mouth with the back of his hand like an insolent teenager.

"I can stay by myself," Maddie interjected, giving him the side-eye.

"No way."

"My friend Emily in Bozeman stays by herself all day while her mom works at the phone company."

"You're not Emily."

She scowled. "Nobody's gonna murder me."

"I know. Because you're not staying by yourself."

Maddie slumped down in her stool, her skinny shoulders rounded. Instinctively, he wanted to reach out and hug her. But since she'd come to Marietta, she'd been distant, aloof. He knew she needed to talk about their mom. It wasn't healthy to keep it all bottled up inside. But Tanner was a shitty communicator at best, even with his baby sister whom he loved with all his heart.

Flo shook her stiff head and made a tsking sound. "It's a hard age. You want to be so grown-up, but you still need some looking after."

Tanner remembered the age all too well. Hard didn't even begin to describe it.

"Why don't you hire a babysitter?" Flo asked.

Maddie looked up, horrified.

"Sorry, hon. Not a babysitter…more of a nanny."

No better, according to the look on Maddie's face.

Seeming to realize she was digging herself into a deeper hole, Flo struggled out of it. "Not a nanny. You know, a *companion* of sorts."

Tanner rubbed his thumb over the condensation on his glass. "I've thought about it, but it has to be someone I know. I don't want her with just anyone."

"I'm not a baby," Maddie said, pouting.

"Nobody said you were. But I've got a lot of jobs lined up this summer, and I need to take damn near all of them if I want this business to take off. I don't want you sitting in front of the TV for three months until…"

Maddie looked up, her hazel eyes bright behind her smudged glasses. "Until Aunt Vivian comes to get me?"

The expression on her small face killed him dead. The way her bottom lip was tucked underneath her slightly bucked teeth. The way her chin trembled just the tiniest bit, like she didn't want Flo to see the sudden emotion there. Tanner knew how this grief thing worked. He'd been living it, too. It rose and receded like lapping waves. One second you were fine, and the next you weren't.

Flo, bless her heart, patted Maddie's hand. "I'll just leave you two alone. Let me know if you want a refill on that milkshake, sweetie."

Maddie watched her go, clearly miserable.

Tanner pushed his plate away and leaned closer to his little sister. She had both hands wrapped around her mug as if it might fly away.

"Hey."

She didn't look over. Just stared at the milkshake with tears welling in her eyes.

"I know you miss Mom, Mads."

The sound of the diner hummed around them. The low murmur of voices, an occasional laugh and the scrape of utensils on plates. But Tanner was only aware of his baby sister. So tender, so vulnerable to all the things that could hurt her in this world.

"Where's my dad, Tanner?"

The question cut him like a razor. It was a good one. Maddie's dad had been no-good, just like Tanner, Luke and Judd's dad had been no-good. They'd been emotionally abusive assholes who'd consumed Jennifer Harlow, and then left her despondent and alone. Along with four children wondering what they'd done wrong, why they hadn't been worthy of love from the men who should've cared the most.

It was a question Tanner struggled with to this day. Only he was able to push it aside now. Able to bury it underneath work and life, and day-to-day bullshit that helped numb him some.

Maddie wasn't old enough to do that. She was still asking questions about her dad. But what bothered him the most was that she'd eventually ask more. Like, why hadn't their mother protected them? Why had she let those losers into her life? Why had she been so incapable of learning, and of putting her family first?

His childhood came rushing back then. Like the waves of

grief, it came in waves, too. He thought of seeing Francie Tate that afternoon, and how that had opened a fissure inside him that had been sealed for a long time. She was just as gorgeous and sweet as she'd been in high school. He'd always had a thing for her. Hell, it hadn't been much of a secret. She'd probably known all along. That dickhead boyfriend of hers had definitely known.

Sighing, he scrubbed his face with both hands. All of a sudden, every muscle in his body ached. When his gaze finally settled on Maddie again, he tried to formulate an answer in his head. *When you're older, your brothers and I can help find your dad. If you want to find him, we'll help...*

But before he could open his mouth, she swiveled on the stool and faced him. "I don't want to go live with Aunt Vivian," she said, pushing up her glasses. "I want to stay here with you."

"Maddie—"

"You can take me, Tanner. You and Judd and Luke. You guys can take me."

"Maddie, I don't—"

"I'll never see you if I live in Hawaii! I'll never come back."

"You will come back. I promise. And we'll come there to see you."

Her chin trembled again, this time uncontrollably. "You don't want me."

He reached for her hand, the words ripping him in two. "That's not true."

"Then why are you sending me away?"

"I'm only twenty-six…" *I love you too much to mess this up…*

"So I'm cramping your style?" Her nose was running now.

It was so absurd that he had to stifle a laugh. She had no idea what she was talking about. But could he blame her? He felt like a Neanderthal trying to pick a daisy without crushing it.

"Maddie, I don't know how to be a dad to you right now. I can't even figure out a good situation for you this summer, let alone the rest of your childhood. Aunt Vivian has a big house, she lives in a neighborhood full of kids. She can give you more than I can."

"But I don't *want* her! I want *you*. You could do it if you wanted. You could."

Legally, it was true. Their mother hadn't left any stipulation for Maddie. Of course she hadn't. But Vivian made the most sense. Maddie would be better off with her. In his heart, he knew that. Mostly.

He handed her a napkin and put an arm around her back. Her shoulder blades stuck out like the wings of a baby bird.

"Listen to me," he said.

She sniffed and wiped her nose.

"We're gonna take this day by day. We're gonna get through this week, and the week after that, and the week after that. We're gonna do what's best for you, and what'll give you the best shot, Maddie. You're not going to struggle like I did when I was your age. Judd did the best he could by me, but he was too young to be a parent. We want more for you."

She looked over and opened her mouth, but he cut her off.

"Day by day," he said firmly. "Okay?"

After a long second, she nodded. Such a good girl. As fucked up as their mother had been, she'd managed to get Maddie this far. It was up to him to figure out how to get her the rest of the way.

"How about a refill on that shake?" he asked.

She nodded again and pushed up her glasses.

Chapter Three

FRANCIE STOOD IN the paint aisle of Big Z Hardware and Lumber trying to decide between Autumn Rose and Burnished Tuscany. A fan spun lazily overhead, moving the thick air and cooling her skin.

She sighed. She could really use Audrey's help. Her best friend growing up had become a successful glass blowing artist in Marietta. She'd always had an eye for colors and textures. Instinctively she knew what looked amazing together and what to avoid. Even her outfits in the sixth grade had been gossip worthy, when the rest of the girls had struggled to match their socks to their cable knit sweaters.

Frowning, Francie put her hands on her hips. She should've made Audrey come today. If she wasn't careful, she'd end up with an orange bedroom.

"Hi."

Startling, she turned to see a girl standing behind her. Baggy shorts, a faded Taylor Swift T-shirt, purple framed glasses sitting low on her nose.

Francie smiled, recognizing her from the other day. *Maddie Harlow.* Tanner's little sister.

"Well, hi there."

Maddie smiled back and the effect was adorable. She was tall. Almost as tall as Francie, and so slender that her arms and legs looked like the appendage equivalent of noodles. She reminded Francie of every middle schooler who hadn't blossomed yet, who was still struggling to find their way. She reminded her of Tanner. And just like that, her heart gave a weird little lurch.

"We were at your house last week," Maddie said. "My brother is your landscape guy?"

"Of course," Francie said. "Maddie, right?"

The girl nodded, looking happy she'd remembered her name.

"Are you here with your brother now?"

"Yeah. He's looking at shovels, I think. Or something dirt related."

"Oh, yeah?"

"He's earthy and stuff," she said, making air quotes around *earthy*.

Francie had to bite her tongue to keep from laughing. There was a spark in this little girl. Something special underneath all the tween gangliness that shone bright as an evening star.

"Ah," she said. "I get that about him. What about you? Are you liking Marietta so far?"

Maddie stiffened. Francie knew now that Maddie and Tanner's mom had recently died. She'd seen the obituary, and some of the folks in town had mentioned it in passing. Jennifer Harlow had lived in Bozeman for the last ten years of her life, but people in Marietta still remembered her.

She watched Maddie bite her cheek and rock back on her worn white Converse shoes. "I like it here. Everyone's really nice," she said. "And Tanner has a dog. She's great. She knows how to sit and speak. I'm teaching her how to shake, but I don't think she knows the word yet. She just paws at everyone for a treat."

"She'll get it. Dogs are smart. What's her name?"

"Charlotte."

Francie's insides warmed. The fact that a man as rough around the edges as Tanner would name his dog something as beautiful as Charlotte made her tingle in all the right places.

"She's very cute. I saw her in the truck with you the other day."

The little girl sighed. "Yeah, we spend a lot of time waiting for Tanner."

"You do?"

"Yeah. He's trying to find someone to watch me. But I don't need a babysitter," she added quickly.

"Oh, I wouldn't think so. But it's probably a good idea. You know. Just to ease his mind."

Maddie considered this thoughtfully. "Yeah...I don't want him to worry or anything."

"Of course not."

"He says they have to be *responsible*," she said, imitating his voice almost perfectly.

This time Francie couldn't help it. She laughed, which seemed to please Maddie to no end. If Tanner needed a nanny, she could always sign up for the job. Maddie was a kick.

All of a sudden, she imagined it. It actually made perfect sense. She'd be working on the bungalow all summer, and Tanner would be spending a good part of it working on her landscape. Since the yard was one of her favorite features of the house, she'd decided to spend most of her allotted savings on it, and tackle the projects she could handle herself.

"I'm sure he'll find the perfect person, and you'll have a great summer, honey."

"I hope so. I miss my…" Her voice trailed off.

"Hey," Francie said, knitting her brows together. "Can I ask you something important?"

The little girl looked wary. Francie spent a lot of time around kids, and she knew they were more intuitive than most adults gave them credit for. Since Jennifer's passing, Maddie had probably been asked about her mother more times than her heart could handle. From her expression, it was clear she thought she was about to be asked again, and Francie could almost see the emotional armor in her eyes.

She nodded toward the paint. "Can you help me pick a color?"

Maddie's face relaxed.

"I'm trying for something rustic," Francie continued, "but I don't want my bedroom to look like the inside of a tangerine."

The little girl stepped forward, her ponytail swinging. "I like this one."

"Burnished Tuscany?"

"Yeah."

"That's the one I was leaning toward, too. You don't think it's too orange?"

Maddie grinned, obviously thrilled her opinion was being considered. "I think it's pretty. The other one hurts my eyes."

"That seals it, then. Burnished Tuscany it is."

"Maddie?"

They both turned to see Tanner standing there, a new rake in his hand. Francie's stomach tightened. Like his little sister, he wore a rock star T-shirt, a preference that must run in the family. But his was a Led Zeppelin number that fit his lean frame just right. His jeans were worn and frayed, and he wore big, thick boots that were caked with dried mud—his badge of landscaping honor.

"Hey," Maddie said. "I saw Miss Tate—"

"Francie."

"I saw Francie and she asked me to help pick a color for her bedroom."

Heat bloomed across Francie's chest. For some reason, Tanner knowing the color of her bedroom seemed intimate.

Tanner's dark gaze shifted, settling on her in a way that suggested he might've noticed the intimacy, too. At least for a second.

"Painting?" he asked.

"Always. But I like it, so that's okay. It's cheap and easy, and things look so much better afterward."

"I like painting, too," Maddie said, looking hopeful.

Francie smiled at her.

"So, we're set for Monday?" Tanner asked. "I'll stop by

and give you the official quote?"

"Monday. Yep." She hadn't forgotten. In fact, she'd been thinking about it almost hourly. "Will you be bringing Maddie? She could come inside and have some ice cream."

Maddie bounced on her toes.

Frowning, Tanner looked down at his little sister. "I'm bringing her. I'm looking for a place for her to be during the day, though, so I won't have her much longer. I think she's sick of sitting in the truck."

"You know, Tanner..." Francie's throat tightened. She was probably going to sound presumptuous. Oh, well. "She mentioned that. You're thinking of a nanny?"

He shot Maddie a look.

"I hope I'm not being too forward," she said, "but if you don't have anyone specific in mind, I could keep her. I'll just be working on the house, and I'd love to have her."

"Wow...I don't know what to say."

Maddie clapped her hands together. "Say yes!"

"Honestly, it'd work out great because you'd be close, right? And she could help me paint."

"I love to paint!" Maddie said.

"You just decided this?" he asked. "Just now?"

She shrugged. "There's not much to decide. She needs a place to be, and I could use the company. It makes sense."

"Are you sure..."

"I'm a teacher. So you know I'm responsible." She winked at Maddie, who grinned at the inside joke.

"Well, you'd definitely be helping me out. I'll pay you, of course."

"Or just take it off my bill. Win, win."

His mouth relaxed into an easy smile, and there were those elusive dimples again. His jaw was peppered with dark stubble, setting off his olive skin and shaggy brown hair in the sexiest way.

She stuck her hand out. "Deal?"

He looked down, his gaze burning into her skin. Then took her hand in his. He was warm and strong, his fingers long and lean. As hot as he was, she was utterly unprepared for the jolt of electricity that followed. It heated her blood. Made her heart race and her knees weak. Maybe it was the fact that he held on just a few seconds longer than he'd needed to. Maybe it was the look on his face, knowing, but withdrawn at the same time. Like he was thinking something that she might eventually be privy to.

Maddie bounced forward and slapped both hands on top of theirs. "Deal!" she said.

Chapter Four

TANNER HAD ALMOST forgotten Maddie's birthday. Thank God Judd had called a few days ago to make sure he was planning something. "She's turning twelve, Brother," he'd said, the cell reception crackly from LAX. "And we just lost Mom. You have to make it special."

He stood at the edge of the pasture now and leaned over the peeling white fence. One of his clients, Lou Bianchi, owned a ranch out by Miracle Lake. She had a nephew a little younger than Maddie and they'd hit it off a few weeks ago, laughing and chasing each other around one of the old barns while Lou and Tanner talked bark mulch.

When Tanner had called asking if he could bring her out to ride horses on her birthday, Lou had been thrilled. He'd had to explain that Maddie didn't know many kids in town yet, so it wasn't really a party. She'd only wanted to invite two people, Colton and Francie.

He watched the two kids riding a gentle white mare around bareback, the grass and wildflowers brushing their sneakered feet. The jagged Montana mountains rose behind them, punctuating a sky so blue that it made his heart ache.

Lou had gone inside to finish the chocolate cake. She was

a nice lady with bleached blonde hair, weathered skin, and a belt buckle as big as her head. She was happy that Colton had found a friend. He spent the summers with her in Marietta and had struggled socially in the past. Tanner was glad, too, and smiled as the kids' innocent laughter reached him from across the pasture.

He looked over as a red Volkswagen Beetle made its way down the long, dirt drive. Dust rose behind it like a parachute and Charlotte ran to meet it, barking her head off.

Francie. She'd called to let him know she'd be a little late, but that she was definitely coming. And she wanted to know what Maddie's favorite color was. She was going above and beyond, bless her. Maddie worshipped the ground she walked on and would've been crushed if she hadn't made it.

He watched her park the car and step out into the warm, June afternoon. She wore a simple white sundress that accentuated her smooth, tan shoulders. The sun hitting her hair had the effect of giving her a halo, and his groin tightened as he took her in. Not an unfamiliar reaction. In fact, it seemed like he'd spent half his life reacting to Francie Tate in one way or another.

She bent and scratched Charlotte behind the ears with one hand, while holding a pink, glittery gift bag in the other. Jesus, she was beautiful. He'd been infatuated with her since he'd first seen her in her volleyball uniform their freshman year. Ponytail bouncing, adoring crowd cheering her name. The team captain and pint-sized dynamo, who loved everyone and who was loved in return. Her mom had been Miss Montana and had groomed Francie to follow in her stiletto footsteps.

He'd never had a goddamn chance.

Seeing him, she smiled and waved. She'd never been crowned Miss Montana like her mom. But she'd been crowned homecoming queen, which was just as good in Marietta. Back then, Tanner thought he'd loved her. But damn, she'd wasted all that beauty and sweetness on scumbag Guy Davis. To Tanner, she'd sold out. Lowered herself to his level. If he was being honest with himself, some of that old resentment still churned when he looked at her.

Watching her make her way through the grass, he knew that wasn't quite fair. If it had been once, it wasn't anymore. She was grown now, her rhinestone tiara long since put away in some dusty drawer.

He recognized the way she looked at him, though. Like she was seeing him for the first time only now. He'd grown up, too. But he was still the same guy he'd always been, just without the stutter and wimpy arms. Why couldn't she have seen him all those years ago? There was a part of him, some small part, that *wanted* to make her want him, if only to relieve some of that old teenage angst and frustration. To show her what she'd been missing all along.

But the question was, if he spent any kind of meaningful time around Francie Tate, ex-homecoming queen, girlfriend to the star running back, would he be able to keep his wits about him this time? He sure as hell hadn't when he was fifteen, when his heart lay somewhere in that gray area between pure and jaded.

She smiled as she got closer. A butterfly flew around her

head and she deflected it with one hand. Charlotte followed adoringly at her feet, falling in love with her just like everyone else.

"I hope I'm not too late," she said. "Looks like the kids are having fun."

He reached out and took the gift bag, careful not to touch her fingers in the process. Protecting himself in some small way from the power she had over him. But he could smell her perfume well enough, and it made his chest constrict.

"Thanks for coming. I owe you one."

"Are you kidding?" she said, peering between the slats in the fence. "I wouldn't miss it."

He stood there towering over her, and looked into the pasture, too. Maddie seemed content for the first time in weeks. Her cheeks, which had been sunken and pale before, were now full of color. She'd even gotten a tan from working in his yard. He'd assigned her petunia duty, which she took very seriously. He now had petunias coming out his ears, but what the hell. If it made her happy.

"Twelve, huh?" Francie shook her head. "One more year and you'll have a teenager on your hands."

He swallowed hard, watching Colton lead Maddie around on the swaybacked mare, pulling her along every time she stopped for a mouthful of grass. "My aunt will have a teenager on her hands," he said. "Maddie's going to live with her and my uncle in Hawaii at the end of the summer." He hated how the words sounded coming out of his mouth, but this was reality. The sooner he faced it, the better.

Francie glanced over. "Oh…I didn't realize."

"It'll be better for her. She'll be happy there."

She looked back at the kids in the pasture and it was quiet except for the calling of a whippoorwill in the fragrant pines behind them. "I'm no expert," she finally said. "But she seems pretty happy here. At least, I know she will be until fall. You're doing a great job with her, Tanner."

He laughed. "It's only been a few weeks. I haven't had time to mess it up yet."

"It's a big responsibility. I heard your brothers are coming back indefinitely."

"They're working on it. For a while at least, until she leaves. And then we'll figure it out. Go out to see her as much as we can, and she can come here for the summers…"

Francie nodded, but didn't say anything.

"I'd keep her," he said, "but my life right now… It wouldn't be fair." He didn't know why he was trying to explain it. But he liked Francie. He'd always liked her, and whether he was comfortable with it or not, her opinion mattered to him. He didn't want her thinking he'd just give up on his sister.

"You don't have anything to feel guilty about," she said, quietly. "You love her, that's obvious. And she loves you. I guess it just makes me sad. The circumstances."

He let the words settle. It was sad. But at least they were still a family unit. Screwed up and a little weird, but a family unit nonetheless.

She looked back over, and this time he turned, too, his gaze settling on her. He remembered looking at her in class, watching how her hair moved over her collarbone when she laughed, how her ears turned rosy at the tips when she got embarrassed. There was a time when he knew her face better than his own. He would've done anything for Francie Tate back then. But he'd been a stupid kid. Too open and naïve. He was tougher now. And a hell of a lot smarter.

"You'll figure it out. You've always been strong, resourceful," she said. "I remember that from high school."

His muscles went rigid at that. His hands, which had been clasped easily over the fence, twitched. That wasn't true. He'd been a joke.

"Come on, Francie," he said, unable to keep the bitterness from his voice.

Pushing off the fence, she turned and gazed up at him with that signature, sweet-as-apple-pie look. She was still used to speaking and having people hang on her every word. That was so like the girl he used to know. But when it'd really mattered, she hadn't used that quiet spunk to move out from under other people's influence. At least she hadn't all those years ago. If she'd changed, if she could tell everyone to go to hell now and still be comfortable in her own skin, he wouldn't know, would he? Because he didn't *really* know her anymore.

"What?" she said. "I'm telling it like it is."

"Telling it like it is? Give me a break. I sat in English and let Guy throw things at my head."

Her face colored. He didn't want to be talking about this shit. It was humiliating, but she'd brought it up. And now he was pissed.

"He was an ass," she said.

"Yeah. I know."

"And you were just young. You hadn't found yourself yet."

He laughed again. Now, that was genuinely funny.

She planted her hands on her hips. "What?"

"I'm sorry," he said, "but you're stretching it. Let's call a spade a spade."

"You were *sweet.*"

"I was a pussy."

"You weren't!" She was getting worked up, which was something he could get used to. The tops of her breasts flushed where they swelled over the heart-shaped neckline of her sundress. She looked hot to the touch. "How can you say that? You let Guy have it that day in the gym."

"I let him have it? I tackled him and fucked up my own knee. Had to have surgery a year later."

"And you also broke his nose…"

"By default. The bleachers actually did that."

She scowled, frustrated. There was a small furrow between her brows that he hadn't noticed before. Then he realized it was because he'd never seen her *frustrated* before. He wondered what other emotions she was used to keeping in check. Anger? Passion? Jealousy? The list was a mile long. Suddenly he pictured peeling her layers back, until he got to what really made her tick. What was she hiding deep down? And was it worthy of all the adoration she'd gotten her entire life? He had a feeling it was. But the truth was, he'd probably never get that far. The vulnerable Francie would be even more dangerous than the perfect one. And honestly, he didn't have time to fall for anyone right now, much less a woman who made him want to rip his hair out and kiss her senseless at the same time.

"Well, I guess I don't remember it like you, then," she said.

"No, you wouldn't." His tone was cool. "Because your reality was always skewed."

She flinched. Maybe he'd hit a nerve. Maybe he should feel bad about that. But one of those layers was being peeled away right before his eyes, and he was too curious to feel bad about anything at the moment.

Her lips pursed until they practically disappeared, and all of a sudden he itched to pull her close and push the flimsy straps of that dress down until it slid all the way to the ground. He guessed she wouldn't be so mad then. Not by a long shot.

"What's that supposed to mean?" she bit out.

"That you were sweet. Maybe a little too sweet. You always saw the best in people when sometimes there wasn't anything good to see."

"I'm assuming you mean Guy?"

"I mean a lot of people. Guy…me. Everyone was a project for you, Francie."

"And that's why you think I stayed with him?" she asked. "As a project?"

"I don't know why you stayed with him, honestly."

Sensing the change in his voice, Charlotte hung her head and slunk over to sit at his feet.

Francie frowned. "See? Now you're upsetting your dog. *And* me."

"I'm sorry. I didn't mean to upset you."

She crossed her arms over her chest and stared up at him. "Do you *always* say exactly what's on your mind these days, Tanner?"

"I never say what's on my mind. You have a strange effect on me."

"Thank you?"

He felt a slow smile tug at the corners of his mouth. And then she smiled, too. Her eyes were clear and blue in the fading light of the afternoon. Her lashes as long and dark as a doe's. She was the girl next door, the all-American teenage dream. She'd grown up, but had she changed where it really counted? He couldn't seem to resign himself to the fact that it shouldn't matter, anyway. She was a friend from his past, if you could call her that. She was a client. She was his little sister's nanny for the summer. That was it.

"Y'all ready for cake?" Lou called from the porch. "My grandmama's recipe! Come and get it!"

Tanner waved. "Thanks, Lou!" He looked back down at Francie then. "Hope you're staying for cake."

She narrowed her eyes, and he thought her shoulders straightened a little. He'd picked at her about as much as she'd allow for today, he could tell. Maybe she'd decide to leave if she'd had enough. Or maybe she'd stay, even though he'd opened a wound between them. Something that might need to bleed a bit before it would heal.

"I wouldn't have it any other way," she said.

Chapter Five

FRANCIE PRIED OPEN the paint lid and set it aside on the
plastic drop cloth. Then she stood up beside Maddie
and looked down with her hands on her hips.

"There it is," she said. "Burnished Tuscany. What do
you think?"

Maddie smiled, pushing her glasses up. "It's super pretty.
It reminds me of fall."

"It's awfully orange."

"I like it."

"Okay. Ready to get our paint on?"

Maddie jabbed her roller in the air. "Ready!"

The draft blowing on their shoulders was cool and delicious, thanks to Tanner. He'd come over and fixed her
window unit, so the painting job ahead was more of a treat
than tedious. At least that's how she felt with Maddie beside
her, in all her tween excitement.

She gazed out the window to where he was currently
chopping back the wisteria. A monstrous job that made his
thin, white T-shirt stick to his back. It was a nice view, she
had to admit. He'd turned his baseball cap backward and his
dark hair stuck out underneath, dripping with sweat.

Francie kept sneaking looks, something that Maddie was starting to notice.

The little girl grinned. "You can take the lemonade out to him before we start, if you want."

"What? Oh. That's okay. When did we decide to take it out? Noon?" She looked at her watch. "It's not even eleven yet."

"He looks pretty hot, though."

"He does. He does look pretty hot."

Maddie giggled.

"Okay, Miss Maddie," Francie said, smiling, "you take that wall, and I'll take this one over here." She reached over to her vintage transistor radio on the windowsill and flipped it on. Something crackly and Garth Brooks came out, filling the room with a country song that reminded her of elementary school.

Maddie dipped her roller in paint and began tackling the wall, her arms reaching almost as high as Francie's. Her hair was pulled back into its signature ponytail, swinging busily behind her as if it, too, had a job to do.

Francie watched her for a second, enjoying the moment, quiet in its simplicity. She had painting company. She had a strong, hunky man working in her yard. And despite what that nagging voice of reason inside her head told her, she looked forward to the fact that it was a big job. That he'd committed to several weeks of juggling her place, along with his other clients', too.

Francie didn't exactly have a full social calendar since moving back to Marietta. She had Audrey, who was always a blessing. And she had her parents, but that was it. Truthfully, she'd been lonely. Tanner and Maddie showing up had been the sweetest, most unexpected gift. Even if she was still trying to figure this new Tanner out. The grown-up who was so markedly different than the teenager. He was stoic, sexy, brooding. But there was also something else deep down, and it had something to do with her, she could feel it.

He'd held a mirror up in front of her face the other day, and she hadn't liked it.

She moved the roller up and down, as Garth crooned from the windowsill. She hadn't let herself think too much about what he'd said, because whenever she did, her heart beat a little faster. Her palms grew slightly damp. It was weird that those old high school memories made her anxious. Because she wasn't in denial or anything. She wasn't. And then she'd remind herself that she'd simply done the best she could, and she breathed easier again.

Maddie bent to put more paint on her roller, her bangs flopping over one eye.

"So, how's it going, honey?" Francie asked.

"Okay. Look! I'm almost done with this side. I mean, we'll have to do another coat, but still."

"It looks great." She paused and pushed her hair away from her face before continuing again. "But I meant, how's it going? In general, I mean. Here with your brother?"

"Oh." The little girl stood on her toes and rolled over the bare spots with the paint. "It's going pretty good." She looked over and smiled, tiny orange spatters freckling her nose. "Thank you for watching me this summer."

Francie's heart twisted. How many times had she been tempted to take Maddie into her arms since she'd met her? More than she could count. But she was careful to keep her distance, careful not to push where physical affection was concerned. She didn't even know if Maddie was the cuddling kind. Maybe she'd rebuff a hug, resenting the implication she was a baby. Twelve was a complicated age. The body was growing, but the heart was still so tender.

"I'm just happy you'd want to hang out with me," Francie said. "And you're even helping me paint. I'm pretty lucky."

Maddie pulled up her shorts with one hand, but they sagged again immediately. She was like a baby horse.

"I love to paint," she said. "Tanner helped me paint my bedroom once when I was little. Bubblegum pink." At that, a shadow passed over her face. "I remember because my mom was going to do it, but she had a fight with my dad."

"Oh. I'm sorry."

"They fought a lot. He was always mad." She shrugged her thin shoulders. "But Tanner hung out with me when my mom couldn't. He helped build forts for my stuffed animals when they were fighting. He protected me."

The words were gut wrenching. *Protected her.* From how many things was Tanner able to protect his baby sister? And how old had he been himself? Just a baby, really.

"He's a good big brother," Francie said, trying to keep her voice even.

"The best. All my brothers are. They moved out when I was a baby, Luke and Judd did. But they always bought my school clothes and stuff like that."

The little girl was slowly painting a picture of what her childhood had been like under the care of her mother, and it was stark. Francie thought about her own mom, so obsessed with perfection and smiles, and weekend beauty pageants. It couldn't have been a more different upbringing, yet she couldn't help seeing a similarity that she would've had a hard time admitting to anyone else. Her mother hadn't ever *seen* her. Not really. And it sounded like Maddie's hadn't, either.

She looked out the window to where Tanner worked. He faced the house, so she could see his expression clearly enough. Serious concentration as he negotiated the plants, shaping them, molding them, like the artist he was. There was a shadow of a beard along his jaw, and the ropy muscles in his forearms flexed as he reached up to cut down a particularly thick vine. This man, the one who looked so fierce doing his job now, had built stuffed animal forts with his little sister as a teen. To distract her. To protect her.

She remembered him in freshman English, how she'd been furious at Guy's behavior, but how she'd gone on to her second period class, able to forget it. Able to tuck it away, so it didn't taint the delicate bubble around her perfect little world. Because she was the beauty queen and Guy was the star athlete. It was just how it was supposed to be. Tanner had been a side note. Something to trouble herself over, if only briefly, so she could live with herself later. *Like a project?*

And there it was again—that anxiety that had risen in her throat the day of Maddie's party. The day Tanner had confronted her with things she didn't necessarily want to remember. That made her want to stomp her foot and shake her head. *I didn't do that! You're remembering it wrong!*

But if she was guilty of distorting reality, so was he. He was wrong when he said he hadn't been strong. He was. She remembered that part clearly. It was a quiet strength that had been smoldering underneath the surface the whole time. Until it had eventually sparked and caught fire that day. That day in the gym.

She could see the blood gushing from Guy's nose, the rage on his face. He'd been a big kid for his age with broad shoulders and a thick neck. He must've outweighed Tanner by forty pounds. But he'd underestimated the smaller boy's spirit. And how tired he was of everyone's bullshit.

Francie looked over at his little sister now, so sweet and gawky. Her ponytail was spattered with paint now, too, and there were a few drops down the front of her tank top.

After hesitating a second, Francie reached out and rubbed her back. Maddie turned, and for one brief moment, she wondered if it had been a mistake. Francie was a shameless hugger. It had taken adulthood and becoming a teacher to appreciate not everyone was. Especially not every child.

But Maddie's lips curved into a grin. Underneath the thick lensed glasses, her deep hazel eyes smiled, too.

"You know what?" Maddie said.

"What?"

"I bet Tanner would want some lemonade now. Can we take a break and have a glass outside?"

Francie looked out the window to where the bright Montana sun bathed the yard in its warm glow. Charlotte was lying in the shade, snapping at a fly. Someone else was crooning over the radio now, something about love gone wrong. And the house felt like home, truly home, for the first time ever.

Turning back to Maddie, she tossed her roller on the drop cloth. "That's a good idea, kid. Let's hit it."

TANNER SAT ON the porch swing next to Maddie, rocking back and forth in the balmy, summer evening. The sun had gone down, leaving the sky a grainy purple, and the air a little cooler against their skin.

Maddie picked up her Sprite, and the ice clinked in the glass. It was the only sound except for the squeaking of the swing, and it made Tanner nostalgic for evenings like this when he'd been little. When his mom had been between boyfriends, and had been a presence in his life. She'd liked porch swings. It was the reason he had one now.

Kicking her flip-flops off, Maddie brought her long legs up to cross them, and jabbed Tanner in the side with her knee.

He gave her a look, then laughed and gazed back out to the dark mountains in the distance. "If those legs don't stop growing, we're gonna have to put a brick on your head."

"Think I'll be as tall as you?"

Surprisingly, she didn't seem worried by the thought. He was glad. She seemed comfortable in her skin, at least for the time being.

"Maybe. And then I'll have to teach you how to play basketball so you can get a full ride to the University of Montana."

She fell quiet just as some crickets started yammering in the hibiscus to their left.

He looked over. "What?"

"Don't you mean the University of Hawaii?"

Sighing, he leaned his head back and stared up at the sky. "Mads…"

"I'm not arguing," she said evenly. As if she'd already accepted it. Which made him sad. "I'm just saying…it'll probably be Hawaii. Won't it?"

"Absolutely not. Not if you don't want it to be. You can come back here for school. You can even live with me."

"I want to live with you now."

He didn't know what to say to that. Vivian had called the other day and he hadn't called her back. He told himself it was because he'd been busy working.

"I know you do." He left it at that. He couldn't lie and say it was going to be just fine. Because it'd be hard. An adjustment for everyone. All Maddie had ever known was Montana and her brothers, who'd always carved out time to see her. Vivian was a loving woman, but she hadn't been a constant presence in their lives. She'd been older than his mom by about ten years, and had moved to Hawaii with her husband when Jennifer was still in junior high. It was only now that she was coming forward, and even though Tanner knew it would be the best thing for Maddie, he also knew there was a significant amount of obligation there, too.

Maybe even guilt for their aunt. She'd never been able to save her youngest sister. But she could raise her little girl—give her a good and decent childhood.

He swallowed, his tongue suddenly dry, and pushed a hand through his hair.

"Tanner?" Maddie's voice was faint. There were so many things she might want to talk about. That she *needed* to talk about, and hadn't yet. He was so out of his depth here.

"Yeah?" He turned, and her silhouette was soft in the dusky light.

"Colton asked if I could go to a movie. Can I?"

"I don't…a movie?"

She nodded.

"Like…a date?"

"*No.* Like a movie."

"Just the two of you?"

She nodded again.

Shit. He had absolutely no idea what to say. Yes? She was only twelve. *She* might not think it was a date, but Tanner had been twelve once, and he sure as hell knew Colton thought it was a date. And boys on dates did stupid things.

He cleared his throat.

"It's not a date, Tanner!"

"Colton's a good kid…"

"I know."

"But I don't feel comfortable letting you go alone."

She watched him, hesitant.

"How about I ask Francie to go, too, and we'll sit away from you guys? You won't even know we're there."

Maddie contemplated this. She worshiped Francie. If Tanner had suggested he take them solo, she'd already be throwing a fit by now. Besides, the thought of sitting next to Francie in the dark for two hours wasn't the worst thing in the world. Not by a long shot.

"Like, how far away?" she asked, slapping at a mosquito.

"Like, *totally* far away."

She laughed.

The crickets chirped. Charlotte scratched herself and her tags jingled. Tanner put his arm around his little sister and caught the scent of baby shampoo. It was a good night. He had no damn idea what tomorrow would bring. But tonight was a good night.

"Okay," she said. "Deal."

Chapter Six

"TANNER HARLOW?" AUDREY said skeptically through the straw in her iced tea.

Francie sat across from her best friend in their favorite booth at the Java Café. They were waiting for Francie's mother. They did this every year—had a girls' lunch that inevitably turned into Francie picking at a sandwich while Loretta Tate talked about everyone in town. Blessing their hearts, of course.

Francie shot her a look. "I'm telling you..."

"Yeah, I know. He grew. But Tanner?" Audrey added another pack of sweetener, her one and only vice, and stirred it around with her spoon. "He was always so...quiet."

"Well, that's because he could barely speak." She looked at the door again. Her mom was late. She loved her, but their relationship was complicated at best, and she wanted to get this over with.

Turning back to Audrey, she touched the scalloped collar of her sheer, white blouse. "Does this look okay?"

Audrey frowned. "Why do you always feel like you have to dress up for her?"

"That's easy for you to say. You always look perfect." It

was true. Even in old, ripped Levi's, and an off-the-shoulder T-shirt, Audrey was breathtaking. Her wavy, dark bob hovered over one eye, and her glossy lips were tilted in that signature mischievous way. Francie blamed the bohemian-chic-artist thing she had going on.

But she was right. Francie still towed the line with her mom. Still did what was expected of her, even as an adult. She envied her best friend's attitude. Audrey knew very well that Loretta would be quietly judging her clothes today, but she didn't care. Or at least, she didn't let it affect her wardrobe choices. Francie, not so much.

"Me?" Audrey said. "You're the beauty queen."

"I was never a beauty queen, remember? I never won squat."

"Shut up. I don't feel sorry for you."

Ignoring her, Francie chose a particularly plump sweet potato fry and popped it in her mouth. Pure heaven.

"Um, speaking of clothes," she said, her cheeks full, "I don't know what to wear tomorrow. Help me." It wasn't exactly a date. Was it? Tanner had asked her to help chaperone something that wasn't quite a date, either. But it was something other than him coming over to work in her yard, so in her eyes, she needed to look cute.

"If this is the guy I remember," Audrey said, "he's not gonna give a rip what you wear. He'll love you regardless."

"I wouldn't be too sure about that."

"Come on."

Francie picked out another fry, this time dipping it in ranch first before putting it in her mouth. "My blue eyelet skirt?"

"That, I like. And why wouldn't he love you? What's not to love?"

She touched her lips, checking for crumbs. "Let's start with the fact that I dated the guy who made his life miserable in high school…"

"There's that."

"I've been thinking about it. Actually, I've been thinking about it a lot these past few weeks." Francie leaned her head back against the booth. "I think he might blame me. Maybe not for Guy, but for how I was with Guy. Does that make sense?"

Her friend watched her steadily. "I think so."

"I mean, I wasn't that bad in school. Was I?"

"Girl, we all were."

"But Tanner wasn't. He was always so sweet. I can't think of a single rotten thing he did to anyone."

"He did break Guy's face." Audrey smiled. "That was pretty great."

"It was, wasn't it?"

Audrey tapped the tabletop with one short, purple fingernail. "Speaking of, I saw Guy at Grey's last Friday. He's still got a thing for you, I'm disgusted to say."

Francie made a face. "Gross."

"Says he wants to have coffee. Catch up."

"Double gross."

"But you'll probably go because you can't say no."

The door to the café opened, but this time Francie didn't look over. "Ouch?"

"I love you," Audrey said. "But you do avoid saying no a lot. You know that."

The words stung more than she'd care to admit. "I guess so. Maybe."

"Maybe? Come on, Fran. You're always so worried about making everyone happy."

"That doesn't mean I'm going to have coffee with Guy Davis."

"I'd hope not. Especially since you light up like a firecracker whenever you mention Tanner."

Francie straightened, her cheeks warm. "I do not."

"Tanner? Tanner who?"

At the sound of the soft voice, both women looked up to see Loretta Tate standing there in an elegant, pale pink pantsuit and strappy stiletto heels. Her silky blond hair fell in ripples past her shoulders, and her makeup was flawless, as usual. She was the poster girl for Miss Montana, even all these years later.

She leaned down and kissed Audrey on both cheeks, European style.

"Loretta…" Audrey threw Francie a quick look. "We didn't see you standing there."

"Well, obviously." She turned to Francie. "Hi, honey."

"Hi, Mom." Francie scooted over for her mom to sit.

Loretta eyed the sweet potato fries warily. She didn't do grease. "Sorry I'm late. Your dad's doctor appointment ran late."

"How is he?" Francie asked. "I was planning to come by tomorrow and bring some banana bread, but maybe I should make it this afternoon?"

Loretta picked up a menu and raised her brows. "No salads?"

"Mom…"

"He's fine. A little tired, but fine. He's looking forward to seeing you." She glanced up and smiled at Audrey, then shifted her gaze to her daughter.

Francie knew that look. She braced herself.

"Honestly, Francie," she said. "Why don't you tell me about your love life anymore?"

"I…"

"Tanner who?"

Francie shifted uncomfortably in her seat. She was too old for this. "Mom."

"Tanner who?"

She knew her mother well enough to accept that she wouldn't let this go. Far from it. They'd probably be discussing it at Christmas. She sighed and ran her hands over her thighs. "He's just a friend. I'm watching his little sister for the summer."

"His little sister?"

"Their mom died recently, and he's keeping her until she goes to live with their aunt in Hawaii."

"Oh, how awful." But Loretta's expression suggested she was chewing on that. Like a bulldog. "Is he from Marietta?"

Francie's stomach tightened, and she glanced at Audrey who appeared just as pained. Tanner's family hadn't exactly been from the right side of the tracks. Loretta would never be unkind to someone's face. That was tacky. But what she said behind their back had always been fair game.

"He is."

"What's his last name?"

She raised her chin a fraction. She hated this line of questioning because of where it would lead. She was defensive of Tanner. But at the same time, her mom's judgements carried weight. That's just the way she'd grown up.

"Harlow," she said.

Loretta's dove-blue eyes widened as she connected the dots. "Jennifer Harlow's son?"

"That's the one."

"I'd heard she'd died. Such a rough life, though. I'm not surprised."

Francie adjusted her napkin on her lap and wished she was getting a root canal instead.

"Are you two…" Loretta cocked her head as if she were studying a chemistry problem. "Seeing each other?"

"*No*. No. We're just friends." They were just friends. But would it be so terrible if they were more? As far as Loretta was concerned, she already knew the answer to that.

Her mom watched her for a few more seconds, her eyes intense. "Oh. Because when I came in, it sounded like you might be."

"Well, we're not."

"It's okay, honey. I'm sure he's a nice guy." Loretta ran a hand down one impeccable wave. "But he's been through so much. You know."

"I know. Bless his heart, right?"

Her mother remained stony faced for a moment, then

cracked a smile. "Am I that bad?"

All of a sudden, Francie felt tired. Her mom couldn't help it. She was a product of her mother, and her mother before that. Francie silently swore to herself over her plate of sweet potato fries that someday she'd step out from Loretta's shadow and be her own woman. Even if it meant breaking ranks to do it.

But as far as Tanner was concerned, it didn't matter what her mom thought anyway, because she was determined not to fall for him. Or his little sister. Maddie would be in Hawaii by September, and Francie would be at the helm of a brand-new teaching job in Marietta. Tanner's business was quietly taking off, so who knew where he'd be by then? They'd reconnect this summer, and then they'd move on with their lives. As they should.

She picked up her own menu and decided immediately on a big, fat BLT.

"What are you thinking?" her mom asked softly.

The café was full of people now, coming in for lunch and coffee, and the smell of both filled her senses. Her stomach growled and her hands tightened on the menu. *Would you love me even if I wasn't your perfect little girl anymore?*

"We're just friends," she said, straightening her shoulders. "That's all."

TANNER WATCHED MADDIE and Colton walking up ahead. They were talking about something video game related—

Maddie's voice light and airy, and Colton's breaking every now and then.

Man, puberty really sucked balls.

Francie walked beside him with her hands in her cutoff pockets. The smell of popcorn wafted through the warm summer evening to reach them a half a block from the movie theater. It was a Saturday night, so people were out in droves, passing on the sidewalk and driving by with their windows down and music playing. It was the kind of night he remembered as a teen, wishing he had someone to go out with besides Luke, who always wanted to drag him to the shooting range. The kind of night he'd sit thinking about Francie and what she was doing. Or who she was doing it with.

And now, here she was. Walking beside him. So close that their elbows bumped every now and then. So close that he could smell her perfume, light and subtle, mixed with the scent of the flowering baskets lining the streets.

She turned, smiling at something he said. She looked absolutely stunning tonight, even though he knew that wasn't what she'd been going for. She barely wore any makeup, and her hair, normally sleek and fine, was tousled and sexy. Like she hadn't thought much about it before leaving the house.

She nodded toward the kids ahead. "You think he likes her?"

"I *know* he likes her."

"Think she likes him back?"

"Probably. She gets all weird when she talks about him.

And she's been playing this God-awful music and stands in the shower for, like, an hour at a time."

She laughed. "Well, that might not mean anything. I've been known to waste some hot water in my day, too."

He immediately pictured warm, soapy torrents running down Francie's body. It wasn't necessarily the first time he'd pictured it, but it was the first time she'd given him the idea herself.

"Yeah, well," he said. "She's usually got her head in the clouds. But this week's been ten times worse. I think we can thank our friend Colton for that."

"Can't blame her. He's cute."

"Is he?"

"You know he is." She elbowed him in the side. "You're just being protective."

"Well…she's my baby sister."

They walked in silence for a minute. Most of the shops had their doors open, and people wandered in and out. One couple walked between them, distracted by their ice cream cones, and laughed sheepishly as they passed.

"I have to tell you something, Tanner," she said, when they came back together.

He glanced over, wanting to kiss her like he had all those years ago. But also wanting to know her, too. And that was new.

"What?"

"I admire you. What you've overcome. I know it couldn't have been easy."

He didn't know what to say to that. She was only trying

to be nice, but he stiffened anyway. She couldn't know that no matter how many years passed, or how much space he tried to put between himself and that awkward, stuttering kid, it was never enough. He hated that part of his life because it represented everything he couldn't be, all the things he and his siblings didn't have growing up. But here was Francie, someone who had no problem with the past because it had been kind to her, and she to it.

"Remember when you volunteered to read that passage of *The Catcher in the Rye* in Mr. Conley's class?" she continued. "And you could barely get through it?"

"I remember."

How could he forget? It had been at the height of his stutter, right before the incident with Guy in the gym. But he'd loved that book, and he was sick and tired of his tongue not functioning. Of his throat closing up like a crocus at midnight. And reading aloud in Holden Caulfield's own words seemed like the most liberating thing he could think of at the time. Holden believed in the inherent goodness of man. It was something Tanner wanted to believe in, too.

Everyone had laughed. Except Francie. She'd looked at him with those bright blue eyes. Almost looked right *into* him in a way that had sliced to the bone. It had been a breaking point.

Maddie and Colton stopped up ahead and were looking at something on their phones. Francie stopped, too, and turned, forcing Tanner to face her.

"I remember, too," she said. "Every single word. I remember how you didn't care what everyone thought."

He gazed down at her, standing so close that he could've pulled her to him if he'd wanted. Or bent to put his lips on the hollow of her throat, where he could see the pulse tapping. "I didn't care what everyone thought. I only cared what you thought."

She swallowed. He could see that, too. Clearly, just as he could see that her eyes had grown a little misty.

"It took guts," she said. "What you're doing with Maddie now? That takes guts, too."

He glanced over at his little sister. They were almost to the movie theater. He didn't even know what they were seeing. Something with a Disney Channel star in it whom Maddie loved. There were posters of the actress all over Maddie's bedroom. Apparently she'd dated one of the guys from One Direction, and the fact that Tanner knew this wasn't lost on him. In fact, they'd discussed it in great detail over pizza the other night.

He clenched his teeth before looking at Francie again. "But it doesn't take guts to let her go, does it?"

"It's the best thing for her. You said yourself."

"Sometimes I think it is. And sometimes I lay in bed wondering what the hell I'm doing."

She frowned. "What do your brothers say?"

"Not a ton. That we'll figure it out when they come home next. But I don't know when Luke will be able to swing it. And Judd's flying overtime right now. We all agreed on this, but they're not crazy about it either."

"But you'll get to see her a lot, right?"

"That's the plan."

"And how does Maddie feel?"

He rubbed his chest. "She's pissed. She wants to stay. Thinks Marietta's the best place she's ever been. But she's also never stepped foot outside the state before. My mom didn't exactly give her many experiences. Too busy shacking up with the next asshole that came along to care much."

"I'm sorry, Tanner."

"Hey." He smiled wearily. "I lived through it. I'm learning to forgive her. That's what happens when people die."

Francie watched him, her lips slightly parted. He wanted to rub his thumb along them, feel the edges of her teeth against his skin.

A few seconds passed, maybe more. The people walking by on the sidewalk seemed to fall away, the entire town settling into a kind of hush as they contemplated each other. Underneath Francie's new adult exterior, the one who taught third grade and was fixing up her house on a budget, he could see the girl from all those years ago. The mouth was the same, the eyes, the audacious tilt of the chin. And her heart, which sometimes had trouble separating the good from the bad in high school, still beat strong and sure behind that lovely chest.

"Come *on,* you guys!" Maddie yelled. "We're gonna miss the previews!"

It was Francie who moved first. Who stepped forward and reached for his hand. Who smiled slowly, maybe a little knowingly, as her fingers wrapped around his. And he was glad, because he never would've touched her first. He would've gone to his grave with her on a virginal, Marietta

High pedestal. Keeping her at an arm's length for all eternity because Tanner Harlow didn't deserve someone like Francie Tate.

"We can't miss the previews," she said. "They're the best part."

And then, before he could think better of it, he leaned down and kissed her.

Chapter Seven

FRANCIE SAT IN the darkened theater, the air conditioning blowing cold against her arms. But she barely noticed. She was still burning from the outside in.

She'd been kissed before. Many, many kisses that she could hardly remember. Much less, that she'd *care* to remember. But this had been different in every possible way that a kiss could be different. It had curled her toes, had damn near curled her hair.

Her belly tightened now as she thought about it. She'd seen the way he'd been looking at her, and his expression masked nothing. So she'd reached for him. Innocently, she'd thought at the time. But of course, there'd been nothing innocent about it. And now a space had narrowed between them. Something that had been there since the beginning, was no longer perceptible, and she felt his heat, his energy, just as strongly as she felt her own.

Maddie had seen. So had Colton. Her face warmed at the memory of them grinning at the unexpected sidewalk entertainment. But Maddie had especially lit up, as if someone had opened a window for her and she'd been able to see what she'd only guessed before.

Tanner sat beside her now, quiet and still, his big hand splayed across his thigh. Hers was only a few inches away, and it felt like the air between them was charged. She could see him out the corner of her eye, tall and imposing. She imagined coming to a movie as his date, leaning into his side as the lights went out, feeling his arm around her, and that hand moving up and down her rib cage. Maybe his thumb would brush the side of her breast, or he'd lean close and whisper something in her ear.

She took in a deep breath and let it out slowly, staring up at the movie screen. *So much for not falling for him.* Obviously, she was going to have to get a grip. He was working for her. And she was working for him, watching his little sister for the summer. She had to remember that she was a teacher, for God's sake, and needed to show at least a modicum of restraint in Maddie's presence.

Tanner turned to her in the darkness, leaning close enough that she caught the faint scent of his aftershave. Goose bumps popped up along her arms at the feel of his breath against her cheek.

"Five bucks says Colton will pull the old yawning trick," he whispered.

She had to bite her tongue to keep from laughing. Sure enough, the boy was leaning conspicuously close to Maddie. Poor kid. And being watched from the back row, too.

"Maddie won't let him," she whispered back. "Too innocent."

"I don't know. Her profound boy band knowledge suggests otherwise."

She smiled. "You're on."

They shook, and his hand swallowed hers whole. It was warm and rough, the calluses scraping deliciously against her skin. God, he was sexy.

He let go and leaned casually back in his seat, his long legs spread out in front of him. Her heart was still hammering at the touch. How could he look so nonchalant when she felt as though she was going to have some kind of an episode?

She leaned back, too, and gazed up at the screen, willing her breaths to come slower and deeper.

Yeah. She definitely needed to get a grip. And fast.

TANNER WALKED SLOWLY alongside Francie. Stars winked overhead in the grainy, navy-blue sky, and the streetlamps were flickering to life along Main Street. The kids walking up ahead were sipping their Cokes and chattering.

Francie pulled her soft, white sweater tighter around her. She was curvy, painfully feminine, her hair falling in silky ripples down her back. She reminded him of a 1950s pinup model, beautiful and unattainable.

"So, you owe me five bucks," she said. "I called it. She shut him down mid-yawn."

Tanner smiled. "He tried, though. Which technically means you owe me five bucks."

"How about I pay you with lunch? Tomorrow? My place?"

"Tomorrow I'm laying your sod. So that works."

"That sounds dirty."

"Oh, it's very dirty."

She laughed, and he was finding the sound was something he craved. Like coming home to a warm shower in the middle of winter, or sinking your teeth into a burger after being half-starved. It nourished him somehow. He wanted to make her laugh not only to hear it, but to know he was the one invoking the emotion. He wanted to make her do other things, too. Things that weren't nearly so innocent. Things that involved being naked and sweaty in his bed.

He clenched his jaw and shoved his hands farther down in his jean pockets. Kissing her had been a shitty idea, but since when was he in the habit of making things easier? Now he wanted her twice as bad, and where would it end? With Francie, he didn't see a scenario where he'd finally be satiated. He touched her, he wanted to kiss her. He kissed her, he wanted to make love to her. And if he made love to her, where the hell would that lead? Nowhere? Everywhere? Realistically, he knew this wouldn't end well. And it wasn't just a bad idea for his state of mind. It was bad for Maddie's, too. She was already getting too attached to Francie. To Marietta in general. All he needed was to go and screw her up even more.

Still, even as he thought it, Francie walked closer than before, her small frame tucked in his shadow. He ached to put his arm around her and pull her close, but he didn't.

"Thank you for asking me tonight," she said. "I had fun."

"Me, too. Oh, watch out." He touched her elbow and guided her around a hole in the sidewalk.

She smiled. "Next you'll be throwing your jacket over mud puddles for me."

"No jacket. It'd have to be the shirt off my back."

"I wouldn't complain."

He looked over, but she was watching the kids ahead.

"Francie." He reached out and touched her arm, stopping her while Maddie and Colton took a selfie in front of Sweet Pea Flowers, where there was a massive teddy bear in the window.

She turned, her eyes wide. "What?"

"I wasn't thinking earlier. Not clearly, at least."

"Earlier…"

She knew exactly what he meant. But she was going to make him say it. Because the Francie he'd known wasn't going to wade into something that wasn't comfortable and tidy if she could help it.

He gritted his teeth. "You know I'm attracted to you."

She watched him, and God only knew what was going through that head of hers.

"But I'm not in any kind of position to start something," he continued. "With anyone…"

She raised her chin, and he immediately felt like a dick. He was nowhere near as self-assured as he'd like her to believe. For starters, he wanted to wrap his fists in her hair right where they stood. Even if Maddie and her entire sixth-grade class could see. He didn't necessarily want Francie to know that, but he'd overshot and hurt her, he could tell.

"I get it, Tanner," she said. "You're being smart. Responsible. I totally agree."

He nodded slowly. Her gaze dropped to his chest and stayed there for a long moment before she looked back up again.

"We're both busy," she continued. "You've got Maddie, Quaking Aspen. I've got the house to fix up and school starting in the fall. Definitely smart."

All true. All good reasons not to screw each other's brains out.

"Maybe if things were different, right?" Her voice was sweet, like something succulent.

"Yeah," he said. "Sure. If things were different."

A couple approached from down the sidewalk. They were talking a little too loud, the way people did sometimes when they'd had too much to drink. The kids were still taking selfies several yards away. Cars passed, music played, but Tanner had eyes only for Francie. The way she was looking up at him, the way her mouth curved just so, made him want to tell her that he'd lied. He wanted her. He wanted every single bit that she was willing to give. That he was willing to risk his entire world being rocked, if it meant that he could kiss her again and hold her close like he'd wanted to since he was fifteen years old.

"Francie?"

He looked up at the voice behind her. A man walked toward them in the darkness, and something about the way he held himself made Tanner grow cold.

"Out on a Saturday night, huh? Just like the old days."

Francie turned then, too. She was flustered, Tanner could tell. Whatever had been happening between them just now had messed with her composure. Another layer that had peeled away, leaving her new and vulnerable underneath.

The guy slowed as he approached, but his date was having trouble keeping up. She trotted after him and giggled as he finally came to a stop underneath the streetlight. She tucked her arm triumphantly in his, breathless.

And then his features came into focus, and Tanner went rigid. The broad bridge of the nose, the thick, meaty shoulders that time had softened only slightly. The eyes, which were still small and dark, and holding that same sharp glint from before. *Guy Davis.* Standing only a few feet away and smiling at Francie like he'd just stepped off the football field where he'd scored the winning touchdown.

"Guy…" she managed.

Tanner felt the slow, hot rolling of blood into his chest and up his neck. His fists curled in his pockets, his fingers biting into his palms.

He'd seen Guy around town since high school, but they'd never talked or acknowledged each other. In fact, Tanner wasn't even sure Guy knew who he was anymore. He wasn't the same scrawny kid he'd been in first period English. And honestly, up until now, it hadn't mattered. Those days were long gone, and Tanner had nothing to prove. At least, that's what his brain said. His heart, beating like a freight train behind his rib cage, seemed to disagree.

Guy's lips curved. He seemed to be completely oblivious to his date. And he hadn't even glanced at Tanner yet.

"You look fantastic," he said. "I mean, really. Fantastic."

Francie laughed nervously and Tanner's gaze shifted over. He realized in some weird way that he'd been waiting for this moment. This exact scenario to see how much Francie had changed. *Really* changed. It was like a test to see if she'd pass. And then what? Would he finally forgive her for being a typical kid back then?

As if reading his mind, she looked up at him, the expression on her face drawn.

Then she turned to the other man and smiled. Turning it on like always. "Guy," she said. "How are you?"

Guy stepped forward and hugged her, and she slowly raised her arms to hug him back. Tanner's jaw felt like it was going to snap in two.

When Guy finally let her go, he shook his head. "We need to get together and catch up. I'm not going to take no for an answer now."

"Well, I've been busy with my house. You know."

Tanner watched her steadily. The guy was an asshole. He'd always *been* an asshole, and she knew it. There was absolutely no reason to agree to see him, other than her allowing him to control her.

They all stood there, an awkward silence settling among them as Guy continued to stare at Francie.

She cleared her throat and took an audible breath. "You remember Tanner? From Marietta High?"

It was fucking painful, but even Tanner realized an acknowledgement only made sense. Even if it was just to put the poor woman hanging on Guy's arm at ease, since she was looking more and more uncomfortable by the second.

Guy finally looked over then, and Tanner saw with satisfaction that he had to tilt his head back to see his face.

And there it was. Recognition. And it was sweet as candy. The realization that this was the same kid whose life he'd made a living hell in school. *Bingo.*

Francie moved closer to Tanner's side. In a silent show of support? Or possibly because she was afraid he'd rip Guy's throat out.

Guy took a small step back. Maybe subconsciously. Maybe not.

"Sure," he said, his voice a weird combination of cocky and strained. "How's it going, man?"

Tanner felt his lips tilt as he held the other man's gaze. "Good, man. How are you?"

Like a grown-ass adult, he held his hand out for the other man to shake. And he thought the last time they'd touched each other, Guy's nose had been spurting blood, and Tanner's knee had been twisted almost backward.

They shook, Tanner squeezing harder than he should've. But whatever. Really, he was being nice. He could've crushed some bone right then if he'd wanted to.

He let go and put his hands back in his pockets. Guy blinked up at him and wiggled his fingers.

"This is my friend Gina," he said, looking at Francie again.

Gina's face fell at the word friend. *What a dick.*

"We were just headed to dinner," he continued, taking another step back. This time it was obvious. When he was a few feet away, he looked back at Tanner, his lips hardening a little. "Let's grab a coffee soon, okay, Francie?" And there it was. A subtle, shitty, male chauvinist claim to his ex-girlfriend whom he hadn't seen in close to eight years. Just to try and assert some kind of dominance over her. And probably over Tanner, too. The man had the beginnings of a small paunch, but truthfully, he hadn't changed at all.

Tanner felt the pulse skip in his neck. What he really wanted was to finish what he'd started all those years ago. To sucker punch this guy and watch him crumple on the sidewalk. But he couldn't do that, could he? Maddie was watching, and she came first. Not to mention, this was Francie's fight, not his. She was going to have to decide how to handle this, how much of a priority she wanted to give Guy Davis in her life.

He waited for her answer, and realized he was holding his breath.

"I'll have to check my schedule," she finally said, "and get back to you."

Chapter Eight

FRANCIE PICKED UP the tray with the sandwiches and carried it through the house, pushing open the screen door with her foot. Maddie came bounding up the porch steps to take it from her.

"Tanner!" she called in her high-pitched voice. "Lunch!"

It was overcast, with storm clouds gathering in the east. The air was heavy and muggy, and matched her mood perfectly. Ever since they'd seen Guy last night, Tanner had been quiet and withdrawn. They'd walked back to his truck afterward and she'd looked over at him in the moonlight to see his jaw working back and forth.

He hadn't said much on the ride back to her place and had dropped her off with barely a good night. Obviously, meeting up with Guy had affected him. And why wouldn't it? It had affected her, too. Ever since seeing him, she'd had a sour feeling in the pit of her stomach. She should've told him what exactly he could do with his cup of coffee. And it didn't involve drinking it. She'd hated everything about that stupid encounter—how he'd acted so possessively toward her, how he'd been so dismissive of his date. And how he'd looked at Tanner, with such teeth-grinding superiority. Of course, he hadn't had the nerve to give him that look until he was out of punching range, she'd noticed.

But had she told him to screw off? Negative. Because her mother had ingrained manners and cheer, even if it meant biting through her tongue to deliver. She realized now more than ever, how ridiculous that was. Tanner had noticed. And she felt like she'd let him down somehow. Let herself down, too.

She walked over to the little picnic table which sat underneath a big, shady maple in her yard. The pink roses growing next to the picket fence were the most fragrant there, and she breathed deeply while watching Tanner unload the last of the sod from his truck.

Sweat trickled down the back of his corded neck. He wore his baseball cap backward again, something that always made her ovaries ache. She'd gone over and over what he'd said last night. He was being smart putting Maddie first. But that didn't mean deep down the words didn't cut. Because despite everything, despite honesty and common sense, all she could think about was kissing him again.

"Mmm," Maddie said, straddling the bench. "Turkey on white. My fave. How'd you know?"

Francie tugged her ponytail. "Your brother told me."

"I can't believe he remembered."

"I think he makes it a point where you're concerned."

Maddie looked up, taking a sip of lemonade. "You like him, don't you?" she asked, licking her lips.

The question was so abrupt, Francie could only stand there for a second. Of course, she should've expected it. "I do," she said carefully. "But it's complicated…"

Charlotte walked over and nudged Francie's thigh, demanding a pat. She reached down and rubbed the dog's silky ears absentmindedly.

"Why's it complicated? You like him, he likes you. Why don't you go on a date or something?"

The look on Maddie's face was precious. There was absolutely zero doubt where she wanted this to go. If things were only that simple.

"I…"

Her voice trailed off at the sound of a vehicle pulling up to the curb. She looked up to see a blue car boasting a Hertz rental tag idling in front of the house. A brunette with a sleek A-line bob rolled down the window and leaned over the passenger's seat.

"Maddie?"

Maddie's face, which had been almost rapturous a second ago, fell.

"What is it, honey?" Francie whispered. "Who's that?"

Tanner dropped the load of sod he was carrying and wiped his hands on his jeans. He looked toward the car, and then at Maddie.

"Vivian," he said, evenly. "What are you doing here?"

The woman turned her car off and got out, pushing her dark sunglasses onto her head. "Is that all the welcome I get? For a full day's travel all the way to Montana, I'd at least expect a hug."

Maddie turned to Francie and chewed her bottom lip. *Vivian.* The aunt from Hawaii who'd be taking her at the end of the summer… The little girl's expression made Francie want to pull her into her arms and shield her from whatever she was feeling at that moment.

But before she could touch her, Maddie forced a smile and got up, holding her arms out for a hug.

Vivian wrapped her arms around her and kissed the top of her head.

"I went to your house, Tanner, but obviously you weren't home. Your neighbor told me where he thought you'd be. Hope you don't mind. I just couldn't wait to see you kids." She turned to Francie and held out a manicured hand. "Hello. I'm Vivian Craig."

Francie stepped forward and shook it, as Charlotte promptly stuck her nose in the woman's crotch.

"Charlotte, *come*," Tanner growled.

"Nice to meet you," Francie said. "You must be exhausted. Can I get you something to drink?"

"Oh, that'd be lovely." She turned to Tanner and stood on her tiptoes to give him a kiss on the cheek. Then rubbed the lipstick off with her thumb. "I'm sorry I didn't call, but I knew you'd try and talk me out of coming. Good Lord, have you gotten *taller* since I saw you last?"

He smiled, but it was strained. This visit wasn't going to be easy, Francie could tell.

"Think I've officially stopped growing."

"You're enormous. And sweaty." She planted her hands on her hips and looked around the yard. "Jennifer always said you wanted to be a gardener."

Francie frowned. He was light-years past being a gardener. Anyone could see that. He had a degree in horticulture and was launching a successful business with a client list as long as her arm. She couldn't be sure if his aunt was just oblivious, or maybe was baiting him a little. Or both.

Tanner nodded slowly and turned his hat back around so the bill came down low over his eyes. "Never wanted to be a gardener, Viv. Not that there's anything wrong with that. But if that's what Mom told you, she wasn't paying attention."

"Oh, I don't mean you're not good at it," the older woman said. "This is going to look beautiful when you're finished."

"Francie," he said evenly. "Can I use your bathroom to wash up?"

"Of course. I'll get some more lemonade while you're at it."

"I've got an extra shirt in my truck. I'll be right in."

Francie walked up the steps while Maddie showed Vivian around the yard, pointing out the flowers and different species of plants using their proper names. It was an impressive feat for a preteen, and one she could thank her brother for. Francie couldn't help gloating a little. Tanner was an artist. Pure and simple.

She made her way into the kitchen and stopped at the sink, looking out through the sheer, white curtains to the little girl and her aunt in the yard. And then to Tanner, who walked back toward the house, carrying a wadded-up shirt, with Charlotte trotting along at his heels.

After a second, she heard the screen door slam and the

sink running in the bathroom. She knew he was conflicted about sending Maddie to Hawaii in September. No matter what he said about it being the best thing for her, it was obvious a good part of him wanted her here in Marietta. From what he'd said, Luke and Judd felt the same way. But they were all single men, who worked full-time and hadn't exactly had the best example of domesticity growing up. Keeping her here probably felt like a long shot at best. Irresponsible at worst.

Frowning, Francie opened the fridge and took out the pitcher of lemonade. The ice tinkled merrily in the glass, sounding like summertime itself. She poured a cup for Vivian, before setting it on the counter and looking toward the bathroom again.

He was going to need some support these next few days. Even if it only meant an ear to bend. Tanner was maybe one of the most stoic people she'd ever met, but that didn't mean he wasn't in pain—from the fresh loss of his mother, to the decision against raising Maddie.

All of a sudden, she wanted to see him before he went back out there. At the very least, she was his friend. And she wanted him to know he wasn't alone.

She made her way through the house, her flip-flops slapping softly against her heels. The bathroom door was ajar and the light was on, casting a gentle yellow glow into the hallway. Thunder rumbled in the distance, the trees outside beginning to shiver in the breeze. The windows were open and it blew in warm currents against her skin.

"Tanner?" She knocked on the door and waited.

Silence.

"Tanner...are you in there?"

After a long moment, she slowly pushed the door open. He stood at the bathroom sink, shirtless. He'd wet down his hair, which was slicked back and dripping down the back of his neck.

She actually had to remember to breathe. Had to remind herself not to stare. His body was that stunning. Long, lean muscle and smooth, tan skin. His jeans rode low on his hips where a worn leather belt only accentuated the sexiness.

Their gazes met in the mirror and at that moment all she was aware of was the warm and immediate pulse between her legs. He'd cleaned up, but she could still smell the musky, primal scent of sweat and man. Combined with the look in his chestnut-brown eyes, she felt herself falter, trying to find the right words. But there weren't any. She couldn't remember why she'd opened the door in the first place. Something about being his friend...

He turned and leaned against the sink, his clean shirt still in his hand. She let her gaze drop again, where it seemed destined to be. To his defined chest, to his nipples, small and hard as stones. To the dark line of hair that ran down his abdomen and disappeared underneath his jeans.

He watched her, waiting. The air between them almost crackled, as thunder rolled in the distance. This time closer. The dishes in her china hutch rattled at the low vibration, and the house seemed to be waiting, too.

Again, she forced her gaze up to meet his. He was quiet, as dangerous right then as a serrated blade. She wanted him to reach for her. Maybe push her up against the wall, so she could feel every inch of his length against her body. Never in her life had she experienced such raw, heated desire— imagining things that would've made her mother lock her up until she was thirty.

Blinking, she licked her lips, trying to pull herself together. But his gaze only shifted to her mouth, and her lips began to tingle.

"I..." She swallowed, hyperaware of how his thumb moved over the Formica counter in slow half arcs. Thick veins snaked over his hands, his fingers long and blocky. God, she wanted those hands on her. Roaming, exploring, taking what they wanted. "I just wanted to see how you were doing."

He watched her, his eyes hooded. He didn't seem phased by the tension between them. In fact, he seemed completely at ease, in his element. Making her suffer, little by little.

"Are you planning on seeing Guy again?" he asked.

"Guy? I don't..." The question was abrupt. Apparently, he wasn't planning on beating around the bush.

"Yeah," he said. "Guy."

She licked her lips again, wetting them. Apparently that was going to be her new nervous habit around Tanner. And she wasn't used to having many nervous habits.

"I don't know."

"You said you'd check your schedule."

"Well, I didn't know what else to say. I didn't want to be rude."

His eyes narrowed at that. And somewhere deep inside,

her defenses went up.

"Why?" she asked.

"He's a dick."

"I know that. But I dated the guy…"

"Doesn't mean you have to go out of your way to see him now."

She crossed her arms over her chest, aware that her cleavage was on full display in the low-riding tank top. His dark gaze dropped to take it in. *Good. Give him some of his own medicine.*

"Aside from the fact that you don't like him…and I get that, believe me," she said, "why do you care? You just gave me a lecture on how you didn't want to start anything with anyone, remember?"

"I said I'm not in the position to start anything. I didn't say I don't *want* to start anything."

She cocked her head. "And what does that mean exactly?"

"It means," he said, pushing off the counter and looking down at her breasts again, "that I'd like to start something with you just fine."

That did it. Her cheeks burned. Along with that delicate, pulsing spot between her legs. "You can't say that to me…"

"Why?"

"Because," she managed. "You might think I'm a *good* girl, but that doesn't mean I'm not human. I want it, too." The words embarrassed her. They exposed everything she felt at that second, and that wasn't her style. She was used to holding her cards close, so she didn't fall too hard, or too fast. The question was, would Tanner catch her if she went ahead and let go?

He reached up and ran his fingers along her collarbone. She flinched, her heart thumping wildly in her chest. He was standing so close, she could see the tiny points of stubble on his chin and upper lip. If he didn't shave, he'd have a thick, sexy beard in a few days. And all she could think of was how that would feel scraping against her skin.

"I've always wanted you, Francie," he said, his voice hoarse.

She was about to have complete and utter heart failure. Her breath hitched once, then twice as she struggled to maintain her composure.

Lightning flashed outside the window and the lights flickered. Thunder followed, and Francie had trouble differentiating the rumble outside from the storm unfurling inside her body.

He focused on her mouth again and leaned down slowly. She watched him get closer, could actually feel the heat coming off him. Or maybe that was just her, standing there burning like a match.

And then the screen door slammed, and footsteps pounded into the living room.

They both froze and stared at each other.

"Francie!" Maddie called. "It's starting to rain and the windows are down in your car!"

Willing herself to take a deep breath, she let it out evenly before calling back, "Okay, honey! I'll be right out."

One corner of Tanner's mouth curved. "Saved by the

bell."

Would she call it that? Because her lips were still antici-pating his touch. Aching to feel his tongue nudge them open. It wouldn't have been like last time, a quick, heated kiss on Main Street. This time he *might've* actually pushed her up against the wall, God help her.

Instead, he shook out the T-shirt he was holding and pulled it over his head. She watched his beautiful chest disappear underneath it, and then his muscled abdomen with that dark line of hair running down, down, down...

He tucked the front of it underneath his belt—hastily, not caring, but managing to look more gorgeous than ever.

Pushing a hand through his wet hair, he stared down at her.

"Better go roll up those windows," he said. And then leaned closer, his lips tilting in that way that made her want to reach for him. "Before we do something we might regret."

Chapter Nine

THE WORST OF the storm had passed, leaving only a steady rain beating against Francie's living room windows. Tanner could hear her in the kitchen, cleaning up from lunch. She'd insisted on Vivian staying, too, and they'd all moved inside to eat at her kitchen table, a get-together that she'd managed to make warm and welcoming, despite the tension Tanner knew he was putting out there.

He ran his hands down his thighs now and leaned back on the couch, stretching his legs in front of him. Vivian was telling Maddie about Hawaii, how much she'd love the beach and all the kids on her street. And his little sister would look at him every now and then, the expression on her face sad. He couldn't believe she wasn't excited about going at this point. Shit...*Hawaii*? But Maddie had always been a sensitive little soul, and deep down, he knew she wasn't yanking his chain when she said she wanted to stay in Marietta.

"Your uncle Rob can take you parasailing," Vivian said. "Are you afraid of heights?"

Maddie shrugged, forcing a smile. "I don't think so."

"That seals it, then. You'll be a natural."

Tanner watched his aunt, so perfectly composed, all dressed up, even for a long, tiring trip halfway across the country. So different from his mom, that a wave of unexpected emotion washed over him. She'd been screwed up, but he missed her. And his aunt was just doing the best she could.

And then, the ache in his chest grew warmer, warmer, until he started feeling…what exactly? He'd gone over and over this in his head. So many times that he could hardly think straight anymore. Maddie would be happy there. *Fact.* He wasn't prepared to be a father. *Fact.* But still, despite everything, the look on her face made him question it all over again.

Vivian glanced over, taking a long sip of her coffee. "Now, Tanner," she said, putting it down again. "Tell me about this little business you've got going."

He prickled but had to remind himself that she meant well. She didn't know Tanner as an adult. Not really. And whatever his mom had told her had obviously been bullshit. Had Jennifer Harlow really known what he'd wanted more than anything else? Even though she'd witnessed him putting himself through college to achieve it? He doubted it.

Francie came in and sat down a few feet away, but he didn't trust himself to look at her. Just her sheer presence brought things to the surface that he wasn't necessarily comfortable with. Things that confused him. And more confusion was the last damn thing he needed right now.

"It's called Quaking Aspen," he said evenly. "Landscape design."

"And it's just you, right? Nobody working under you?"

"Just me. For now."

She nodded, considering this. "And you're trying to make a go of it? This yard business?"

"I am."

"But you can't have too many jobs, can you? Right here in Marietta? It's such a small town."

Francie leaned forward. "I can tell you, Mrs. Craig, that he's already in high demand. Tanner knows more about botany and design than anyone I know."

"Is that right?"

"I heard just a few days ago that an assistant for the governor was interested in his work."

He looked over. He hadn't mentioned that to anyone.

"Word travels fast in Marietta," she said, glancing back.

Tanner had to work not to smile. She was definitely posturing. Defending him like a little boxer. He only wished she were as tough where that piece of shit Guy Davis was concerned.

"You're a hard worker," Vivian said, her gaze settling on him again. "I'm not surprised. You were always tenacious when you set your mind to something. I've never seen anyone with as bad a stutter as you had, Tanner. And now look at you."

He shifted in his seat.

"I mean it, honey," she continued. "Your mom waited too long to finally get you help. It was shameful."

His ears were hot. "Vivian…"

"You've come a long way." She patted Maddie's knee.

"But we're all lucky Uncle Rob and I are able to step in. There's just no way you'd be able to do this by yourself."

His ears were throbbing now. "I'm grateful you're both here for us, and that you love Maddie as much as Judd and Luke and I do. But I could do it by myself. And would, if that's what it came down to."

"Oh, I know you *would*. But that's not the question. It's whether or not you'd be able to do it the way it should be done. A little girl needs a stable home environment, parents who'll be there for her—"

"I'll always be here for her. I'm here for her now."

"It's true, he is," Maddie said, looking closer to tears than he would've liked.

He needed to stop. To rein this in while he was still feeling civil. He had no idea why he was arguing with his aunt, anyway. This was a done deal.

Vivian put an arm around her and pulled her close. "I know he is, sweetheart. He's a good big brother. But you need a mom and dad."

She'd always needed a mom and dad. She'd never had a complete family, and even now, she was being denied it by the person who'd promised to protect her at all costs. He didn't know what the hell was wrong with him. Why did he want this fight so badly? But he felt it churning in his bones just the same.

Francie, probably sensing his mood, scooted closer. Her smooth thigh only inches from his hand. He needed to get out of there. To think. To calm down.

Clenching his jaw, he leaned forward and put his elbows

on his knees.

An uncomfortable silence settled over the room. The rain continued pounding against the windows and Charlotte snored softly at his feet.

"You know," Vivian said, running her hand over Maddie's hair. "I'd love to take my niece for some ice cream. Is that okay with you, Tanner?"

"Sure. I need to run home anyway." He glanced over at Francie. "I forgot my good sod cutter. Stupid."

She nodded, looking worried.

"I'll be back, okay? The rain should let up by then." But it was obvious he was just looking for an excuse to leave. They probably all knew it. Especially Maddie, who usually jumped up and down at the thought of ice cream, but sat there now, overly quiet.

He'd get his shit together and come back in a better frame of mind. He'd make sure Vivian's bed was made up and the refrigerator was stocked. He'd summon the maturity he needed to get through this visit. To get through letting Maddie go, period.

When he stood, Charlotte snapped her head up and stood, too, shaking herself off.

"Thanks for lunch, Francie." He looked down at her, in the simple cotton tank top and cutoff shorts. And felt a pull so strong that it spooked him.

Definitely needed to get the hell out of Dodge.

FRANCIE PACED HER living room floor. Back and forth, chewing on her nail and glancing repeatedly out the window. The rain was still coming. Steadily, in miniature torrents against the glass. Tanner couldn't work on the yard in this. Which meant he wasn't coming back any time soon.

She stopped and crossed her arms over her chest, feeling the chill of the empty house all the way to her toes. Maddie had gone with her aunt to get ice cream, and the absence of the little girl and her brother, and even his sweet, long-legged dog, made her more lonesome than she'd care to admit.

Tanner had been in a strange place when he'd left, she could tell. His aunt seemed like a nice person with only the best intentions, but the way she spoke to him was almost like she expected a custody fight. Would he give her one? He'd made it pretty clear this arrangement was fairly set in stone, even if he and his brothers weren't thrilled about it. But the look on his face this afternoon, the one where he seemed to be coming right out of his skin, said otherwise.

She stared out the window to where his truck had been parked only an hour ago. She could still see the heat in his eyes from before, when he'd stood in the bathroom with water dripping from his dark hair. She could still feel his pent-up energy. He'd reminded her of a caged tiger.

And then, without thinking it through, pushing away every single reason why it wasn't a good idea, she leaned over and plucked her keys from the end table and walked out the door.

Chapter Ten

TANNER OPENED HIS fridge and took out a beer. Touching the rim to the edge of the counter, he smacked it with his palm and watched the top fly off with a satisfying *thwack*!

He raised the bottle to his mouth and took a long, frothy pull. His aunt obviously didn't think he'd learned anything useful in college. She should watch him pop the tops off longnecks. It was a beautiful sight.

Taking another drink, he walked into the living room and sat on the arm of the couch. The house was quiet. Too quiet. His shoulders were so tight, he could feel them strain against his T-shirt.

He licked the tangy porter from his lips, and the taste reminded him of the first time he'd gotten drunk. He'd gone back to his dorm room with a pretty brunette named Fae, but he'd fucked up and called her Fran. She'd never returned his calls after that. Go figure.

He'd been hung up on Francie, even when he'd thought he was done being hung up on her. It seemed as though she'd followed him around all these years, looking over his shoulder, reminding him that nobody was ever going to live up to that perfect, homecoming-queen image.

Charlotte pricked her ears toward the door, then let out a yip. Craning his neck, he looked out the window, and saw Francie's little red Beetle at the curb. *What the hell...*

He stood and headed for the door, his boots thumping heavily, purposefully on the hardwood floor. There were a dozen reasons she could be showing up. She was sweet, sensitive. And it didn't take a clairvoyant to have seen how unsettled he'd been leaving her house. Still, deep down he knew that wasn't why she was here now. They had unfinished business. Maybe she didn't realize it yet, but he did.

He opened the door to see her standing there with her fist raised mid-knock. Jesus, she was easy on the eyes. Her hair was damp from the rain, hanging in sexy, messed-up strands past her bare shoulders. Her tank top was wet, too, and see-through as hell. She wore a lacy white bra underneath.

He forced his gaze up and leaned against the doorjamb, still holding his beer. He didn't trust himself to speak. His throat had gone dry.

She smiled and lowered her hand. "I just came to check on you," she said. "You left so fast..."

"You noticed that, huh?"

"Kind of hard not to."

"I was feeling claustrophobic. My aunt's...problematic."

She watched him. "She doesn't understand you, Tanner. That's obvious."

"I don't think she ever did. Here..." He stepped aside. "Come in."

Lowering her head, she walked past, and he caught her scent. Shampoo, a trace of perfume.

She patted Charlotte, who greedily nudged her hand, and looked around. "Your house is beautiful."

"Thanks. Didn't come this way. It's taken a few years."

All of a sudden, he saw it through her eyes. The crisp, clean lines of the 1950s ranch. The midcentury modern style that screamed bachelor, unattached. Even his furniture was less for comfort and more for the eye. But it hadn't taken long for Maddie's influence to take over. Now there was a fuzzy pink blanket thrown over the couch and a few soft pillows nestled on the chairs—things she cuddled up with when she watched TV.

He was proud of his house. Like Quaking Aspen, it had been a labor of love. It made him happy to see the admiration on Francie's face.

She turned to run her fingers down the period brick mantel, and he let his gaze fall where it wanted. Her long, tan legs. Her ass, which practically begged to be cupped in a man's hands. Her hair—that golden, unruly mass of waves that he longed to touch.

He set his beer on the coffee table and straightened to lace his hands behind his head. "Why did you come over here, Francie? Really?"

She stilled. Then turned to face him. "To check on you. Why? What do you mean?"

"I mean, I think we're dancing around something here. And doing a pretty shitty job of it, too."

"I'm not dancing around anything."

"Really?" He dropped his arms to his sides. "Why didn't you just call, then?"

"I…"

He took a step toward her, the sultry summer rain pulsing against the house. "You, what?"

"I don't know. I guess I wanted to see you."

"After what almost happened at your place?"

She shrugged, looking away. He could tell, even through the damp curtain of hair, that her cheeks were pink. Probably hot. He wanted to cradle her face in his hands, run his thumbs underneath her lashes. He wanted her looking up at him and saying his name. The Francie he'd always known wasn't shy. Far from it. So what was it about him that was making her blush like this?

"I know what you said before," she muttered, "about being responsible…was right. But I guess I just wanted to be impulsive for once. Even though it might not be the best thing. Or the safest thing."

She looked up then and he'd been right. Her cheeks were a bright, throbbing pink. And the color was stunning on her. "I did want to check on you, though," she continued. "But maybe that wasn't all of it…"

They watched each other as the seconds ticked by on the old grandfather clock on the mantel. Something he'd bought at an estate sale because it reminded him of stability, if that wasn't the most boring thing in the world. But the passing of time had always held a strange kind of comfort. No matter what transpired in life, it was there in the background, steady and reliable. Even now, the sound of that ticking grounded him. Which was a good thing, because the look on Francie's face didn't.

He took a step closer, then another. He didn't want to think about what she'd just said about responsibility. He didn't want to think at all. And when it really came down to it, maybe he'd never had a chance in hell where keeping his hands off her was concerned. It was like holding back the tide or harnessing a blizzard. Maybe he'd been powerless to it all along.

She watched him, her eyes bright. Francie Tate was standing here in his living room, her lips parted, her skin flushed. Her chest rose and fell with shallow, nervous breaths. Breaths that said she wanted him as much as he wanted her.

"Tanner..." she said.

And then he reached her. He slid his arm around her waist and pulled her close. Her body was soft and giving. Her breasts were warm, generous mounds against his chest.

Bending, he breathed against her neck as she tilted her head to the side. The delicate line of her jaw led into the curve behind her earlobe where a small diamond stud sparkled. Slowly, slowly, he touched his lips to her skin, not trusting himself to move any faster. He breathed in her scent which made him think of everything he'd ever wanted up until this moment. Everything had always led right back to Francie.

She reached up and put her hands in his hair, making a soft sound that lit up every one of his nerve endings.

"Tanner," she whispered again.

Before he could try and talk himself out of it, he bent and picked her up, cradling her against his chest.

She stared up at him, her eyes dark, her lips wet and glistening in the dim light of the room. And then he kissed her. She opened her mouth, her warm, wet tongue flicking against his. She reached up, her fingertips playing at the nape of his neck, moving through his hair like she had a doctorate in how to make men crazy. He realized with a sudden moment of clarity, that she held his heart in her hands now. That she had the absolute ability to crush him where he stood.

Slowly, be broke the kiss and pulled away. He'd been so careful since growing out of that quiet, stuttering boy in school, to protect himself. He didn't get close. Ever. It was the safest way to ensure he wouldn't experience any of the pain his mother had invited his entire childhood. The result was a guy who was closed off from everyone and everything. And now, this afternoon, he felt her chipping away at that wall he'd worked so hard to build, felt it physically falling away, and it scared the shit out of him.

She must've read the look on his face, because she moved her hand to his cheek.

"What is it?"

"You," he said. "It's always been you."

Very gently, he set her back down on her feet. He'd been about to carry her into his bedroom. He'd been about to make love to her, and worse, fuck the consequences like a goddamn idiot. What if she did end up crushing him where he stood? What if she was that same girl from high school with the bouncing ponytail and complete inability to follow her heart because she was so programmed to do what everyone else wanted? He'd bet money that her friends wouldn't want someone like him for her. Much less her parents. He'd always felt he'd never been good enough for Francie. Why would eight years and a house full of nice furniture change all that? So far, she hadn't shown him that he was anything but a novelty, something to play with over the summer. Albeit sweetly.

The bottom line was, he wasn't ready for this. Sex was sex. But this was different, and he knew it.

She looked up at him, confused.

"I don't have a condom," he said. "And this is a bad idea."

"Tanner..."

If she said his name again, he'd come undone. He'd finish what they'd started, and he didn't know if he could take the aftermath.

Leaning down, he kissed her again. This time tenderly, with everything he felt for her, that he'd always felt for her. And then pulled away with the wall surrounding him damaged, but intact.

"The rain stopped," he said. "I need to get back to work."

Chapter Eleven

F RANCIE PULLED UP to her house with her backseat full of groceries, and her heart heavy as a cement block. She put the car in Park and sat there as the wipers moved back and forth over the windshield, the sound monotone and drab.

Her yard was empty in the steady rain, the sod covered with tarps and Tanner's tools sitting underneath the overhang on the porch. The weather had stayed dark and dreary for the past three days, so he hadn't been back to work. She'd kept Maddie a few times, but he'd always made some kind of excuse not to stay, and in the process had left her longing for him more than ever.

They hadn't talked since the afternoon at his house, but he'd made himself clear enough—together, they were trouble. And could she really argue with that? Who said she was ready for some kind of spontaneous love affair with Tanner Harlow? Who said he was ready for one with her? Even though his aunt had left yesterday, she could still sense the heaviness in his mood. The situation with Maddie weighed on him now more than ever. But she also felt something else keeping him at bay. It was as if he didn't trust her, not completely. Ever since they'd seen Guy that night, he'd seemed hesitant. Like she'd start rummaging in her closet for her old cheerleading uniform and go running after her old boyfriend, her old life.

There was a part of her that wanted to bow up to that. But there was another part that understood. To him, she might as well still be that girl, since she hadn't exactly proven otherwise.

Francie watched the raindrops snake their way down the glass, startled when her phone rang. Turning, she fished it out of her purse, and frowned when she saw the screen. *Tanner...*

"Hello?"

"I didn't know who else to call." His voice was strained.

She sat up straighter, her heart skipping a beat. "What is it?"

"It's Maddie. She's okay, but...she's not okay. She's having some kind of meltdown and I can't get her to come out of her room."

She could hear muffled crying in the background. "Oh, no. Will she talk to you at all?"

"No. The last time I went in there she went berserk. Threw a pillow at me."

"What?" She couldn't picture Maddie doing anything close.

"I've never seen her like this. I don't get it."

"Okay, I'm coming over. I have to run my groceries in really quick, but I'll be there in ten minutes."

He exhaled on the other end of the line, clearly relieved.

Tanner was one of the biggest, strongest guys she knew, but right now he was putty in her hands. Which touched her.

"Francie…"

"Yeah?"

"Thank you."

FRANCIE KNOCKED SOFTLY on Maddie's bedroom door, with Tanner a safe distance down the hall. He stood with his hands in his pockets, watching her warily.

"Honey? It's Fran. Can I come in?"

Sniffing. "Francie?"

"Yes, babe."

More sniffing. "Yeah. Come in."

She threw Tanner a cautious look, and he shrugged, staying where he was.

Francie pushed open the door, and her heart squeezed. The room Tanner had decorated for her was a perfect representation of the middle schooler she knew. A purple accent wall, framed posters of Taylor Swift and Ed Sheeran, even a hammock strung up over her desk where a perilous amount of stuffed animals lay hibernating.

Maddie was curled into a ball on her bed, but when she saw Francie, she sat up and wiped her nose with a tissue. It was the first time Francie had seen her without her glasses, and her big, hazel eyes were red and puffy. Her cheeks were colorless and streaked with tears. Whatever it was, it was significant.

"Honey…"

"I don't want to talk about it."

"Okay…but can I at least come sit by you?"

The little girl scooted over and made a spot next to her.

Francie sat, and when she knew Maddie would allow it, wrapped an arm around her and pulled her close.

"I wish you'd tell me what's going on," Francie said. "Or at least give me an idea? Your brother's pretty worried."

"I know. I almost hit him with my pillow. I feel bad."

"Well, I think he could've taken it, but he *is* worried."

Maddie pulled away and wiped her nose again. She seemed to be considering whether or not to say anything else, then sighed heavily. "I'm bleeding," she finally said.

"You're what?" Francie couldn't process the words. She took her by the thin shoulders and looked her up and down. "Where?"

Maddie reached for her glasses, put them on, and then blinked matter-of-factly. "Down *there*."

Bingo… It was all starting to make sense. Tears, meltdown, pillow as a weapon… Francie felt her stomach muscles relax.

"You mean your period?"

Maddie nodded.

"Is this your first one, sweetie?"

She nodded again, her chin trembling this time.

Francie hugged her. "It's *okay*. It's all right. Do you know anything about menstrual cycles, Maddie?"

"We learned about them in health class last year. Gross."

Francie smiled against her hair. Being this age was so

hard. "I know. It's going to be tricky for a while until you get used to it. But you will. And the great thing is that someday, if you want to, you might be able to have a baby because of your period. It's all pretty cool, really."

Maddie sniffed. "I think it's disgusting. And my stomach hurts. And Colton asked if I could go swimming at the lake tomorrow if it stops raining, and now I can't."

"Well, you *could,* if you'd try a tampon—"

The little girl shook her head adamantly. "No way. And I feel pressure to say yes, even though I don't want to."

Something about that was like a punch to Francie's stomach. It sounded all too familiar. Pressure to say yes, to please everyone else.

"Listen…" She pushed Maddie away enough to look at her. "Colton will understand. If you don't feel comfortable this time, it's okay to say no. The people who really care about you will get it. And they'll stick around for next time, okay?"

Maddie nodded, miserable.

"Do you have anything? Any pads?"

She shook her head. "I used toilet paper."

"Oh, honey. Okay. I'll run to the store."

Maddie grabbed her hand. "Don't go yet. Please?"

She was barely twelve. And had no mother to talk her through one of the most important days of her adolescence. It made Francie's throat ache.

"But you need something other than toilet paper. You'll be more comfortable that way, I promise."

The grip on her fingers remained tight, unforgiving.

"Okay…we can ask Tanner to go."

Maddie's eyes widened, but she didn't argue. If she was willing to let her big brother embark on a maxi pad mission, she must've really needed a hug right then.

"Let me tell him what's going on," Francie said, "and I'll be right back, okay?"

The little girl, who was tall and gangly for her age, and who had the softest, sweetest eyes Francie thought she'd ever seen, pushed her glasses up and smiled. Just a little. "Okay."

Chapter Twelve

TANNER STOOD IN aisle five of Monroe's Market, arms crossed, feet planted apart, staring in complete and utter confusion at the products lined neatly on the shelves.

There were pads with wings, pads without wings, thin pads, heavy pads, pads that boasted "flex technology," whatever that was. Francie had specifically promised there'd be something for tweenagers, but he hadn't stumbled over that particular gold mine yet.

Frowning, he rubbed the back of his neck.

"Tanner?"

He turned to see EJ Corpa standing a few feet away. He held a basket full of groceries, with a bottle of wine sticking out the top. Probably for his girlfriend who drove in on the weekends from Missoula. He was always talking about her. They shared a hyper, one-eyed puppy named Wink that Charlotte thought was the Antichrist.

"How's it going, man?" EJ asked, glancing at the pads. The grocery store elevator music played lamely in the background, stretching the moment into infinity.

"Holy shit, dude. I'm lost, here. Do you know anything about this stuff?"

The look on Tanner's face must've spoken volumes, because EJ came over and began studying the display like an algebra problem.

"It's okay," he said, giving Tanner a slap on the back. "We'll get you through. Who are they for?"

"My little sister. Twelve."

"Okay. How active is she?"

"Likes to ride bikes and stuff. She's been riding horses at Lou's lately, too. She likes to swim."

EJ frowned. "That's where you're fucked looking at these things. She needs some tampons."

"I don't think she wants those."

"Better to have them and not need them, then need them and not have them. That's my motto, and I'm usually right. At least about this shit."

They exchanged a look of silent understanding.

"Here." EJ grabbed a couple of pink boxes off the shelf and tossed them in Tanner's basket. "And you'll need some of these. And this. And a few of these wouldn't hurt, either. Remember, if she doesn't use them all now, she will eventually, and then she'll have an arsenal."

Tanner nodded, feeling his blood pressure begin to come back down again. "Thank Jesus you came along when you did. I might've been here until Christmas."

EJ laughed. "We've got to stick together, man. Take care of our girls. That's what it's all about."

"True."

The other man eyed him curiously. "Speaking of girls…"

"I know what you're going to say. You heard about Francie, and we're just friends."

"Uh-huh. That's not what Carol Bingley says."

"God. Carol Bingley says a lot of things."

"Friends don't usually suck face in front of the movies, Tanner."

"Technically, that's true."

"*Technically* that's true." EJ rolled his eyes. "Come on, man."

Tanner took a deep breath and let it out evenly. It was only a matter of time before somebody confronted him about this. And EJ wasn't going to buy any of his bullshit, either. He knew exactly how Tanner had always felt about Francie.

"I can't get involved with anyone right now," he said. "I've got my sister to take care of."

"Yes, you do. But that doesn't mean you have to stop living your life. Last time I checked, raising kids and having a girlfriend aren't mutually exclusive."

"No. But it complicates things."

"Maybe. But don't you think it could be worth it this time?"

EJ knew some of the stuff about Tanner's mom, his history and childhood. He knew it wasn't easy for him to open up, much less to people who had the ability to screw him up emotionally. EJ had a tough past, too, but he'd moved on. Found happiness. There was a part of Tanner, small and tucked away, that admired that.

He squeezed the handle of his basket and looked past EJ to a big banner in the window advertising steaks for 20 percent off on the Fourth of July. The market hummed around them, with people shopping and chatting up their fellow customers. From somewhere up front a checker got on the loud speaker and asked for a price check on cherry tomatoes. The surroundings felt as normal and safe as anything would on a Tuesday night in Marietta. So why did he feel so close to losing it? He knew the answer, of course. It was the mention of Francie. The suggestion that maybe he should trust someone not to be an asshole for once. Maybe settle down into some kind of give-and-take relationship.

But Tanner was a loner. He'd always been a loner, and that's what he identified with. If he wasn't busy being alone, then who was he really?

Clearing his throat, he looked back at his friend. "Hey, man. I appreciate it, okay? But I'd better get back before the shit hits the fan."

EJ nodded slowly, recognizing he wasn't getting through. That maybe he never would. Tanner felt bad about that, he really did. But that's just how it was.

FRANCIE SAT ON the couch with Charlotte and Maddie, a soft pink blanket draped over all three of them. They were watching the Disney Channel—something about twins who were having boy problems. Seemed legit.

Rubbing Charlotte's ears, she gazed out the window to the mountains in the distance. The rain had finally stopped, the gray evening sky giving way to splotches of purples, oranges, and yellows.

Maddie laughed at something on the screen, and Francie looked over and smiled. She seemed to be feeling better. She'd taken an ibuprofen and had changed into some comfy sweats. Tanner had texted a few minutes ago saying he was on his way with "supplies," which made her grin. Overall, she felt inexplicably content in the moment. Which worried her, because this wasn't her family. Far from it.

The front door opened and he walked in with two paper sacks from Monroe's.

He raised his brows. "I take it the coast is clear? I'm not wearing a helmet. Should I go get one?"

Maddie giggled and pushed herself up to a sitting position. "Sorry, Tanner."

"Hey, it's okay. I'm just impressed by your aim."

He looked over at Francie and their gazes locked, an undeniable heat passing between them. Her heart thumped behind her breastbone. He was so handsome, so *rugged*.

Finally looking away, he walked over to the coffee table and began taking out the contents of the bags.

"We've got slender tampons, *just* in case. We've got pads with wings. We've got pads for nighttime with super absorbency. We've got thin liner thingies for a light flow, and…" He pulled out a gallon of rocky road ice cream. "We've got comfort food."

Francie stared up at him. It was like he was a period angel, sent straight from heaven with his menstrual cycle offerings. She honestly didn't think he'd ever looked hotter.

"Can you stay?" he asked. There was a hint of a smile on

his lips, and the crease between his brows had smoothed a bit. It was a small clue as to how he might be feeling. Like maybe he was happy right then, too.

"Stay?" She didn't know what he meant, but her brain skipped ahead about a thousand steps anyway. *Stay tonight, stay tomorrow. Stay indefinitely.*

"For a movie?" Tanner continued. "If we'll all fit on the couch. The dog has to scoot over, though."

Maddie beamed. "Yeah, Francie! Can you stay? It'll be fun."

She couldn't think of anything she'd rather do more.

"Sure," she said. "I'd love to."

AT JUST AFTER eleven, Tanner woke Maddie and walked her to her room. She was still half-asleep and Francie heard him from down the hall telling her to crawl in bed, that one night without brushing her teeth wouldn't kill her. The little girl argued, but not for long because after a few seconds, Tanner appeared in the living room again.

"She's obsessed with oral hygiene. She's gonna wake up pissed tomorrow."

Francie pushed the blanket off and stretched. "You have to admit, that's pretty adorable."

His gaze fell to her chest, before coming back up again. There was something in his expression she couldn't read. Things had grown so complicated between them in just a matter of days.

"Thank you for coming over today," he said. "I don't know what I would've done otherwise."

Her lips tilted at that. "You would've done just fine."

"She can throw me for a loop sometimes."

"She's a preteen. She's supposed to throw you for a loop. That's how you know she's working right."

He nodded. "Good point."

"Today was a pretty big deal," she continued, "and you handled it like a pro, Tanner. Better than my own mom did."

"No ice cream?"

"Are you kidding? I got a lecture about how sugar combined with all my new whacked-out hormones would make me break out. And we couldn't have that." She paused at the memory. At how her mom had sat her down and listed all the things her period meant, including the possibility of gaining weight. And in her house, that would've been like going out and robbing a bank. It stung, even today.

She swallowed hard. Tanner hadn't been good with Maddie this afternoon. He'd been damn near perfect.

"Huh," he said. "Sounds like she didn't realize you were the prettiest girl in school, even with a face full of zits."

"I was never the prettiest girl in school."

He shook his head. "How can you say that?"

"Easy. I was popular because I was part of the *in* crowd. Not the same thing as being an attractive person. Or even a good person."

She'd said too much. She hated talking about how she really felt growing up. With the constant pressure and unrealistic expectations. She still felt it. All of it.

He took a step toward her. Then another, and another, until he stood right over her. He held a hand out, those hands that were so big and capable—rough but gentle at the same time. "Come here," he said.

She watched him for a few seconds, and then let him pull her to her feet.

She felt so safe in Tanner's presence. Like the only thing that might hurt her would be her own heart for letting him in. But looking back, she'd never really stood a chance, had she? From that very first moment she'd seen him standing on her porch in that white T-shirt and those faded jeans, she'd been a complete goner. Didn't matter how many times they reminded themselves this wasn't a good idea, or how it wasn't the responsible thing. From that first day, they'd been tumbling toward this night right here.

His eyes were darker than usual, almost black in the minimal light of the living room.

"What are we doing, Francie?" he asked, his voice low. "I swear to God, I was never going to touch you. I was going to come to your place and work, and never lay a damn finger on you."

They stood so close that she could feel his erection against her lower belly. She ached to touch him there, ached to touch him everywhere, actually. But she stood completely still, afraid he might pull away. And take something with him when he went.

"Don't you know I've wanted you to touch me?" she managed.

He ran his hands up her bare arms, the sharp contrast of his skin against hers, mind-numbingly delicious. A warm, delicate pulse built at the base of her throat, and her legs trembled underneath her.

And without another word, he leaned down slowly, until his mouth hovered over hers.

"You're beautiful, Francie," he whispered. "You were beautiful then, and you're beautiful now. Inside and out."

It wasn't what he said, it was how he said it. As though he meant every word.

Lowering his head, he kissed her long and deep. His lips, which always looked so hard and serious, were warm and giving. She kissed him back, trembling everywhere. He wrapped a strong, steadying arm around her lower back, and she let herself lean into him. Suddenly, the insecurities were gone—they'd flown away like a bevy of doves. In their wake, she felt free, sensual, like a woman who knew what she wanted, and wasn't afraid to ask for it.

Reaching up, she put her arms around his neck and felt his hair tickle her forearms. And then, so quickly she didn't have time to process it, he picked her up. Like the other day in his living room, but this time, he turned and carried her quietly down the hall and into his bedroom. Charlotte padded sleepily behind, but he shut the door before she could follow them inside.

Francie laughed. "Poor, Charlotte."

"She'll live. She goes everywhere with me, but I'm drawing a line here."

"You don't think Maddie will wake up?"

"She sleeps like the dead. I'm guessing we won't see her until after nine. At least."

"So, does that mean I'm invited to stay until morning?"

He nipped gently at her neck, her throat, her earlobes which were unbearably hot. She heard her earring click against his teeth. "You're invited to stay until morning. I might even make you breakfast."

Her heart pounded at that. This was dangerous. He had to be thinking the same thing. The taste of domesticity was sweet as granulated sugar on her tongue. And just like something sweet, she craved it. Had she been needing this all along? Had he?

That was the thing with loneliness, though. Sometimes it masked itself as being busy, or stoic, or guarded, or simply stuck-up. But sometimes, lonely was just lonely. For Francie, it didn't matter how many people thought she was pretty. It only mattered how she felt inside. And lately, that feeling was becoming more and more pointed. Tanner's touch was soothing it some and making her realize what exactly it was that she wanted out of life. To have her own family. To be with them until she was old and gray, and rocking on a swing on her front porch.

Tanner lay her on the bed, and she leaned back against the pillows, staring up at him.

Without saying a word, he peeled his T-shirt over his head. And there it was again, that incredibly fit body that she'd only glimpsed at before. Never touched, even though every cell in her being had practically demanded it. There was only a small lamp on in the corner, and the effect was breathtakingly sensual—shadows that caressed every sharp contour, every long line of his muscled frame.

Smiling, he moved over her like a wolf, taking his time, brushing himself against her, so she could barely keep still. When he came to her mouth, he lowered his head to kiss her slowly, his skilled tongue dancing erotically with hers.

And suddenly, she was someone else. She wasn't the woman she'd come to know, the ex-homecoming queen who painted her house on the weekends and paid her water bill two days early. She was Tanner's, and somehow that made her special. She was fierce lying here underneath him. She had to be, otherwise his energy would've jolted her dead. At that moment, she felt like she could've conquered anything or anyone because of the way she saw herself through his eyes.

Leaning on one elbow, he reached down and unbuttoned her shorts. He breathed against her neck, setting fire to her skin. His knuckles brushed against her bikini line, his hand working the shorts down as she raised her hips off the bed. Down over her thighs they went, until he pulled them off and tossed them in the corner.

He lowered his head to her throat and kissed her there, making his way down to its hollow and then followed the line of her collarbone with his tongue. Gasping, she spread her legs, raising one knee so his belt rubbed the inside of her thigh. She felt him, hard and bulging against her stomach. All she wanted was to be moving naked underneath him. No barriers, nothing but skin on skin.

Seeming to read her mind, he pulled away to look down

at her in the relative darkness. His eyes were black as onyx, his lips tilted in that cocky way that made her want to suck on them.

"I don't think we need this anymore, do we?" he said, tugging on her shirt.

She shook her head, and he lowered himself to her belly and caught the hem between his teeth. He moved it up a few inches, exposing her skin to the chill of the room. She felt his stubble scrape over the sensitive crevice of her belly button, and she moaned, leaning into the pillows.

She felt the warmth of his stomach against hers, the rough line of hair running down his abdomen, his belt buckle, cold and hard against her hip. And then her thin cotton shirt was gone. She lay there in only her underwear, the crotch of her panties soaked through.

Reaching underneath her, he unhooked her bra and moved the straps down, his palms sliding over her shoulders, her arms, and then pulled it off completely. He cupped her breasts in his hands, lowering his head to take a pebbled nipple between his teeth.

She closed her eyes and exhaled slowly, pleasure filling every single nook and cranny, her body responding on its own. She felt her pulse in her ears, in her throat, in the delicate spot next to her groin. Wherever blood rushed, it seemed she was lit with flames that in turn, lapped at her flesh. Hungry and unrelenting.

Finally, she reached for him. His thick shoulders slid seductively underneath her roaming hands. She trailed her fingers down his rib cage, outward over the small of his back, and underneath his jeans to the top of his ass.

He stiffened over her, making a sound deep inside his chest, which only excited her more. Tracing his skin underneath the line of his belt, she moved her hands inward then, toward his lower belly and above his erection that was hard as a brick.

His stomach twitched and his breath caught. She felt the muscles in his long, lean body flex. There was so much male power there. She wondered what Tanner had been capable of all along. He could easily have done worse to Guy in high school, but he'd made a conscious decision not to. Even though he'd had a lot of growing to do, she knew the strength had always been there. The knowledge made her breathe faster, made her stupid heart trip all over itself.

She reached for his belt with shaky hands. He lifted himself enough to give her the room she needed to unbuckle it and pull it through the loops with a soft *swoosh*. She dropped it over the side of the bed, then went to work on the buttons of his jeans. They'd both broken out in a fine sheen of sweat, and the slick friction of their skin was the most primal, sexual thing she'd ever experienced in her life.

She breathed him in, his scent, the fresh scent of his sheets and his house, and she felt herself tumbling, tumbling. Falling head over heels for something she wasn't quite sure she was ready for because she'd have to be ready to lose it, too. And the thought was almost too much to bear.

She pushed his jeans down, and then his Jockeys, until his hot, thick erection sprung free. She felt its velvety length against her thigh and reached down to wrap her fingers around it.

He stiffened and sucked in a breath as she began stroking and exploring. Her heart was pounding so hard that her entire body shook in anticipation.

Leaning over, he opened his bedside drawer and pulled out a condom.

She lifted her head off the pillow to kiss his neck. He was salty and warm.

"I thought you didn't have any condoms."

He grinned in the shadows. "I didn't. But they were the first thing on my shopping list."

"Thank God you're a list maker."

"Right?"

He unwrapped it and rolled it on, then moved her hair aside with one hand, and gazed down at her for a long, tender moment. He didn't try and kiss her, didn't try to articulate anything. Just looked her in the eyes, while she looked right back. She was glad he didn't speak. He didn't have to. She knew exactly what he was feeling, because she was feeling it, too. She was falling in love with him.

Deep down, she knew there'd been no other way for her. It had been going to happen, whether she wanted it to or not. Whether she was ready for it or not. Because love didn't really give a rip if you were emotionally prepared. It came and it conquered. The best you could hope for was that it wouldn't leave a trail of scorched earth in its wake.

Slowly, he pulled her panties down over her thighs, and then, finally, she was naked underneath him. Just as she'd been imagining since that very first day. Except if she was being honest, she'd been drawn to Tanner for a lot longer than that. In high school, she used to think she was unsettled by his dark eyes, his quiet intelligence. But at fifteen, she couldn't have understood what lay beneath that surface. That he would eventually grow into his eyes and would gain control of his tongue to speak to her in ways that would defy logic. He was everything she'd ever been afraid of, everything she'd ever hoped for.

She wrapped her legs around his back and felt him nudge her with his tip. She raised her hips to meet him, hungry and unashamed.

With a groan, he slid inside her. Easy, steady at first. She raised her hips more, wanting him deeper. Wanting him to consume her. Sensing it, he only teased, trailing hot kisses along her jaw.

She thought she said his name, once, twice, but she couldn't be sure. The blood was roaring in her ears now, and all she was aware of was him. Only him.

And then he plunged deep, again and again. Her orgasm built like sparking fireworks in a night sky. Small, crackling flames that she felt from every corner of her body. What had been dark, was now lit with every color imaginable. What had been cold, was now warm. And what had been empty, was now full.

Tanner tensed over her, then shuddered with his own release. He breathed against her neck, and she closed her eyes with an overwhelming sense of love that shouldn't have taken her off guard, but it did anyway.

When their breathing had slowed, he kissed her cheek,

the tip of her nose, her chin, her eyebrows, and then her lips. So sweetly, that she nearly cried because of it.

Pulling away, he looked down at her and smiled. "That was risky, wasn't it?"

She smiled back.

Yes, it was.

Chapter Thirteen

RANCIE'S EYES FLUTTERED open to the first rays of early morning sunlight shining through the slats of the blinds. She rolled over, the warm sheets twisting around her naked body, and looked at the clock. Six thirty. Not as early as she knew Tanner usually got going, because for landscapers, the name of the game in late June was to beat the heat. But early enough, considering how late they'd stayed up having sex. Over and over and over again, before she literally collapsed in his arms, and he fell asleep breathing into her hair.

Her legs were sore, and her lips were chafed. She felt like she'd only now discovered what her body was capable of. And it was a wonderful thing.

The smell of bacon reached her from the kitchen, along with the soft clanking of pots and pans. He was trying to be quiet, not wanting to wake Maddie.

Propping herself up on her elbow, she looked around the room. It was the first time she'd seen it in the daylight. There was a huge bookcase in the corner, where there were too many worn, dog-eared books to count—classics, as well as contemporary fiction, non-fiction, biographies and history journals. Tanner had always been a bookworm. She remembered that as well as anything and thought again about the day he recited a passage from *The Catcher in the Rye* in class.

Several pictures in heavy wood frames hung on the walls—mostly of his siblings—Maddie, with her big brothers. But there were a few of his mother, too. No matter how rocky his relationship had been with her, he still loved her. She knew he was someone whose family meant everything to him.

She blinked up at the pictures, wondering how in the world he'd end up parting with Maddie. *It's complicated,* he'd said. More than once. It was almost like he was trying to convince himself of that very fact. *I can't keep her because of this, and this, and this...*

Rolling over, she reached for her shorts and T-shirt that lay in an unceremonious pile on the floor. It was going to be sunny and warm today—the first day it hadn't rained in almost a week. Which meant Tanner would be coming back to work on her yard. He'd be done soon, which made her unspeakably sad. She'd gotten used to him pulling up in his big, white truck, to Maddie bouncing through the front door, to Charlotte lapping water from the bowl she now kept on her front porch.

Clasping her bra, she frowned, reminding herself that this was normal. This was what people in their twenties did. They hooked up. They had friends with benefits. They could sleep together casually and not expect anything too heavy afterward. But the way she *felt,* though. That was the part that scared her. She guessed it was easy to think you were falling in love with a smoking hot guy at the same time you were experiencing a mind-altering orgasm. But the morning after, that warm, lusty fog should be lifting. At least a little.

She caught sight of herself in the mirror on the back of his bathroom door. Not only did she *not* feel it lifting, but she also appeared to be...glowing? Her cheeks were flushed, her lips were red and tender. And her eyes...there was something about the look in her eyes that terrified her, actually. If he saw this, if he recognized it, he'd run for the hills, and as far away from her lovesickness as he could get.

From the kitchen, there was the clinking of silverware. He'd be coming to get her soon. He'd probably walk through the door, tall and handsome, and freshly showered. He'd lean down to kiss her temple. He'd remind her that he was taking Maddie to Lou's to ride horses tomorrow and would ask her if she still wanted to come.

Her heart ached at that. She knew, no matter how this would end, that Tanner would always be a gentleman. He'd want her to have a connection with Maddie, and he'd want her in their lives in some form or another, at least for a while. Until Maddie left, and things went back to normal. He'd want that, because she knew enough about his childhood, that he detested meaningless relationships. No matter how many one-night stands people their age had. He was different. He'd be a nice guy, and he'd let her down easy.

In Francie's world, men were attracted to her. That didn't mean they loved her. She'd experienced enough to know the difference. Guy had said he loved her. He'd been the first. Since then, there'd been more, and the words had continued to ring hollow and empty. She didn't think

Tanner would say it unless he meant it, but the question was, would he know the difference, too? Would he be able to separate his high school crush from the woman she was now?

She glanced at her reflection again—the long, blond hair, the big boobs. Her looks had only given her a false sense of security growing up that she'd had to slowly accept as her truth. In the past few years, she'd had to turn herself inside out to find the real Francie. And she was still looking.

If this man didn't want more, she'd grit her teeth, raise her chin, and find it within herself to heal and move on. But she didn't think she could do it with a smile. And for the very first time, she felt that was okay.

TANNER WALKED ALONG the dusty trail around Lou's pond and kicked at a rock, watching it skip off into the knee-high prairie grass. Francie walked beside him. She wore a bulky University of Montana hoodie that was doing a pretty good job of hiding her curves. But he knew what was underneath.

In fact, he'd had to force himself to keep his hands in his pockets for the past hour because Maddie and Colton were riding around in the pasture next to them. Within sight. Within hearing distance, for sure.

He looked over at her now and caught the scent of her perfume on the gentle evening breeze. Her hair was pulled into a ponytail, but strands of it kept blowing in her face, and she pushed it away with one hand.

She glanced over. "What?"

"Nothing."

Everything. Truthfully, the other night had blindsided him. He thought he'd been careful enough, at least with his emotions. He had no interest in falling for her any more than he already had, but the temptation to carry her to his bed had been too much. It was as if it had been a script already written for them, a movie that begged to be acted out.

He'd wanted her for so long, but the actual act of making love to Francie wasn't anything he'd been prepared for. He was in deep shit now. And he knew it.

The kids' laughter reached them from the pasture, and he turned to see Maddie jumping the little white mare over a log, while Colton held up an imaginary score card. "Five point two!" he yelled. "I'm taking off points for form!"

"No way!" she cried, patting the horse's neck. "One more time!"

Pulling his phone from his back pocket, he took a picture to send to his brothers. Maddie and Luke had been able to FaceTime a few nights ago, which was rare, and his brother had asked for more pictures. Luke had hung up promising he was going to send her a present made by the local schoolkids, and she'd been excited. He loved kids, always had. Tanner wasn't surprised that he'd managed to make friends with them over there.

Francie laughed, watching Maddie turn the horse around and trot toward the log again. "She's actually really good, Tanner," she said. "She's got a great seat. A natural."

"Oh, yeah?" He squinted in that direction, trying to see

what she meant. All people on horseback looked the same to him. Bouncy.

"Look." Francie leaned close and put her hand on his arm. The evening was on the chilly side, but the warmth of her touch had an immediate effect on how his jeans fit. "See how her body moves with the horse? She's always looking forward, never down. Did Lou teach her that?"

He shrugged. "I don't know. I think she just taught her not to fall off."

She laughed again. "Well, that's a good start."

"How do you know so much about horses?"

"I rode for a while. After high school."

"Why'd you quit?"

"I didn't want to. But I couldn't pay for school and a horse at the same time."

He looked down at her, surprised. "You…"

"Paid for my own school?" Her lips tilted. "Yeah. Why's that so hard to believe?"

"I just thought your parents…"

"I was spoiled, I know."

"Francie…"

"No, it's true. I was. But when it came to college, my mom kind of assumed I'd get married right away like she did. And there's nothing wrong with that. But it wasn't for me."

He watched her. *Another layer peeled away.*

"How'd you do it?" he asked.

"Waited tables. My parents helped with books, so that was more than a lot of kids had."

"Books. Those were a killer."

She nodded.

Something they had in common. Go figure.

"So, now you're a teacher," he continued. "And a really good one, if I know you at all."

She looked away. "I get by."

"Someone like you doesn't just get by, Francie."

She took a deep breath but didn't look back.

Taking her by the shoulders, he turned her gently, so she didn't have a choice. Her eyes were glassy.

"What is it?"

"Sometimes…"

"What?"

"Sometimes it scares me, the things you say."

He brushed the backs of his fingers along her cheekbone, but she jerked away. It was obvious she was trying not to cry, but for the life of him, he didn't know what the hell he'd said.

"What? That you're on another level? You are."

A steely look settled over her features. "Which me are you talking about, Tanner? The teenage me? Or the adult me? Because they're not the same. You *know* that, I know you do. You're even worried I'll go for coffee with Guy, for God's sake."

He frowned, watching her.

"I see you're not going to deny it."

"I know you're different," he said after a minute. "It's mixed up, how I feel."

"I know it is." Her voice sounded smaller then. Tired.

"You feel both ways. You think of me like I was then, and you like that. And you don't."

It was as if she'd opened up his brain, picked out his most precise thoughts, and put them on a tray in front of his face. She was absolutely right. But he hadn't realized it until just now.

"Don't you see?" she said. "You can't have it both ways. You can't keep seeing me as perfect, because then you'd have to accept my flaws. And you're not willing to do that, are you? Not when you'd have to open yourself up a little to do it."

Right then Charlotte came bursting through the trees where she'd been chasing something for the past ten minutes. She ran straight for Francie's crotch, making her laugh.

It was a moment of brevity that Tanner was thankful for. What she'd said was profound. And he didn't have a good answer for her. She deserved one. *He* deserved one. No matter what happened between them, even if it stopped right here, right now, they both needed to make heads or tails of it.

He smiled down at his dog and patted her glossy head. "Where have you been? Rolling in something, by the smell of it."

Francie smiled, too, put her hands in her sweatshirt pocket, and began walking back the way they'd come. The sun was starting its slow decent toward the mountains, and Lou would be waiting at the house with coffee and hot chocolate for the kids.

They fell into step beside each other, and despite the tension that had been hanging over them a minute ago, it was now an easy silence. Francie had a way of doing that. Putting people at ease.

Even the most hardened ones.

Chapter Fourteen

"FRANCIE TATE?"

Other than some background noise, it sounded like Luke was next door. Tanner had to remind himself that his brother was half a world away.

"Yeah."

"Blonde? I remember her," Luke said. "Most of my buddies had a thing for her."

"*Everyone* had a thing for her, dude."

"So...what does she look like now?"

Tanner sat on the edge of his bed with his elbows on his knees. He'd been banished to his bedroom by Maddie who was planning some kind of elaborate surprise. She'd apparently called Francie to come over at seven sharp. Whatever the secret was, it was serious twelve-year-old business.

He looked out the window to the clear jewel-blue sky. It had warmed up again and July was barreling past in a blur of barbeques and leftover firecrackers. Before he knew it, it'd be August. And then September. The thought made his heart beat slow.

The past few weeks had been among the happiest of his life. He didn't want to admit that to anyone, much less himself. What he really wanted was to avoid thinking about it. To bury it deep down and let things happen the way they were going to. But the problem with that was obvious. Maddie would leave soon and Francie would want more. Two things he was going to have to deal with, whether he wanted to or not.

"Tanner?"

He licked his lips and switched the phone to the other ear.

"I'm here."

"So, what's the deal with her? Maddie says you've been spending a shit-ton of time together. Which isn't like you, I might add."

Tanner smiled. Leave it to Luke not to pussyfoot around. "Meaning?"

"You know damn well. Are you falling for this girl?"

"You know how I felt about her in school..."

"This isn't high school, man. You're a grown-ass adult. If you're not that into her, you shouldn't be jerking her around."

"Oh, Jesus. Since when are you the Buddha of relationship advice?"

"Since I had to take over being your mother fifteen years ago, remember? I could never afford to be a total dick where you were concerned. Somewhat of a dick, yes. A total dick, no."

He knew Luke had meant that to be light, a joke more or less, but it wasn't. They both knew it was true. Luke and Judd both had to lead by example. They loved Tanner, and knew he'd always looked up to them. Not having a stable parental figure in their lives, meant the Harlow boys had to learn what they could, when they could, the best they knew how. Even now, all these years later.

"So, how do you feel about her, Tanner?" Luke asked. "Seriously?"

Tanner looked down at his boots, clean because Maddie insisted he wipe them down before coming inside these days. He wondered how much of that she was picking up from Francie, and assumed it was plenty. Francie was rubbing off on his little sister, having a profound effect in just a short amount of time. It was something female, something inherently soft and sweet that he wouldn't have been able to give her on his own. He guessed Vivian would accomplish it, too. But for some reason, he felt cold at that. Would it really be the same?

"Seriously?" he said, his voice low. "I'm in deep here, Brother. Pretty fucking deep."

Luke was quiet on the other end of the line. There was some shouting in the background, maybe his friends playing a game of football on their downtime. It sounded like family. And they were. But at that second, he envied those guys, because his brother was there, and not in Marietta. And he missed him.

"Then what are you gonna do about it?" Luke asked.

"I don't know. I really don't. Maddie's leaving soon. That's about all I can deal with right now."

"Then don't."

"Don't what?"

"Don't deal with it. Don't let her go."

Tanner rubbed his face. His hand was dry and calloused. Too much time outside. Too much time in the sun, trying to make a life for himself. But for what? To end up alone in a house that echoed empty and hollow at night?

"What do you mean, don't let her go? We've talked about this."

"Yeah, I know. But it doesn't feel right."

"It doesn't to me, either, Luke, but it's not that simple. She needs parents."

"Listen." Luke's voice took on the low, authoritative tone of Tanner's youth. "I know that. But you wouldn't have to do it alone. I told you I'm coming home after this tour. Judd's working on it, too. Something permanent. Think about it. Why couldn't we raise her together?"

"What are you *talking* about?"

"We're not kids anymore, Tanner. We're not idiots. Between us, I think we have at least a full functioning brain. Mom, bless her, did a lot worse."

Tanner's thoughts were racing around so fast, he barely had time to catch one before Luke went on.

"I've talked to Judd. He's on board if you are."

"What? When did you talk to Judd?"

"The other day...the other night. Hell, I don't remember. Over here everything runs together. But my point is, we've talked. And now I'm talking to you."

Tanner shoved a hand through his hair. He had no idea how to process this. He thought they'd decided, grudgingly, to send Maddie to Hawaii. Now, he didn't know what to think. Was this actually possible? Could they finish raising her and do a decent job of it? He recognized that he was fairly screwed up. Luke and Judd were screwed up, too. He was scared shitless they'd screw Maddie up by association.

"You don't have to decide tonight, little brother," Luke said. "All I'm asking is for you to think about it. It's a challenge. But I think we're up to it."

"Yeah..." Tanner took a deep breath and caught the smell of warm bread coming from the kitchen. "Maybe. Even assuming we are, Vivian will never go for this. She was just here. She's ready to take her home."

"Vivian wants what's best for Maddie. All we'd have to do is convince her we're it."

"She thinks I'm a gardener."

Luke laughed. "Sounds about right."

Staring out the window, Tanner realized he was holding the phone too tight, and loosened his grip. The doorbell rang, jarring him from his thoughts.

He looked at his watch. Seven sharp. Francie was there, and the feelings that followed weren't unpleasant. They weren't unpleasant at all. At that moment, he realized that half the people he cared about most in the world would be under one roof. And the other half might be home soon.

"Luke?"

"Yeah, Brother."

He swallowed hard at the sudden wave of emotion that threatened to knock the breath from his chest.

"Be careful, okay?"

FRANCIE LOOKED ACROSS the table at Tanner, unable to hide the smile that tugged at her lips. Her cheeks were warm. Actually, they were burning. He seemed to notice, and smiled back, the candlelight flickering across his features.

A homemade pizza sat between them, along with two wineglasses full of apple juice, and a plate of chocolate chip cookies for dessert.

Maddie beamed, untying her apron and taking it off.

"Sweetheart," Francie said. "Did you do this all by yourself?"

"I did. And the cookies are only a tiny bit burned on the bottom."

"Where'd you learn to cook, Mads?" Tanner asked.

"From you, silly. I pay attention when you're in the kitchen."

Francie's heart fluttered. She could picture him cooking for her, getting her ready for school, helping with her homework. And she fell just a little harder then, a little more out of control.

Sitting up straighter, she looked down at Charlotte, who had her head strategically placed in her lap. Probably hoping for a few cookies crumbs. Francie rubbed the soft ears, the pointy head, not saying anything for fear Tanner would make her go lie down on her bed. She was beginning to love this dog and was finding that just the simple act of petting her calmed her nerves. She'd never had a dog growing up. Her mom hadn't liked hair on the furniture.

Tanner shook his head, looking at the pizza. "Well, I'm glad I managed something useful while you've been here."

Maddie walked over and kissed him on the cheek. "You're the best, Tanner. And I love you." She folded up the apron and hugged it to her chest. "Now, you guys eat and enjoy. Lou is taking Colton and me miniature golfing, with burgers after, so I'll be home later."

Tanner stared up at her, his mouth open.

Maddie was clearly enjoying it, her gap-toothed smile just about breaking her face. "Well, I had to make sure you had a first date. You've been so busy taking care of me, you haven't even asked her."

Francie dipped her chin to her chest, trying not to laugh. The whole thing was just about the cutest thing she'd ever seen.

"I..."

"It's okay." Maddie patted his arm. "Mom would say sometimes we have to take matters into our own hands."

"She did used to say that, didn't she?"

Maddie nodded, then came over to give Francie a hug. She smelled like baby powder. Her hair was fine and soft, and as she turned into Francie's ear, it tickled against her cheek. "He really likes you," she whispered. "He might not say it right away, but he does."

Francie felt a distinctive ache building in her throat. The homemade pizza, the sweet little girl, the innocent intention, was all so moving that she had to swallow the emotion down again. She understood now what Tanner had meant about being careful where Maddie was concerned. She'd gotten attached to Francie. She'd seen exactly what was going on between Francie and her brother, and she wanted to foster it. And what was so hard about that, was that Francie wanted to foster it, too. She wanted it to grow like a succulent vine, colorful and fragrant in the summer sun.

Francie hugged her back, not wanting to let her go. But she did, and five minutes later the little girl was out the door and headed with Lou and Colton to the miniature golf place.

She and Tanner shared the pizza, which was cheesy and delicious. They talked about Maddie and how wonderful she was. They talked so much that the conversation rolled back to Tanner's childhood before she really knew what happened. She'd always been careful not to ask too many questions, because she knew it was painful. But tonight, he seemed to want to talk, and she sat back and listened, watching him over the dying candlelight. He told her about how his mother had been a spark who lit up every room she entered, who'd been funny and wickedly smart. But she'd also been selfish and immature, and that was something that would alter the course of her children's lives, as she made one terrible mistake after another.

He talked about his dad and how he hadn't wanted anything to do with his sons, how he'd walked out, leaving Tanner and his brothers with abandonment issues they struggled with to this day. And he talked about life in Marietta. How much he loved it here. How he'd found peace within the walls of his house, and a creative outlet in his business that he'd put all his hopes and dreams into.

He leaned back then and rubbed his jaw, watching her. A

silence fell between them as the sun sank lower in the sky. The light was changing, growing deeper, more golden. And so was the air—cool and romantic as it breezed through the open windows and into the house.

She watched him, too, but it wasn't easy. She was afraid he could read everything that lay in her heart at that moment. He wielded too much power with those dark eyes. That wide, expressive mouth.

"My God," he said. "You really are a beautiful woman, Francie."

Her heart thumped and her chest warmed. In fact, every inch of her seemed to be affected by what he was saying, how he was looking at her.

"It's such a nice night," he said. "Come sit outside with me?"

She wouldn't have been able to say no if she'd tried.

Chapter Fifteen

TANNER HAD FOUND the porch swing at an estate sale last summer. He'd had it in his garage until spring, when he'd dug it out and refinished it, giving it the TLC it desperately needed.

He'd hung it right before his mom died. Right before Maddie had come to stay with him. Up until now, she'd been the only one to sit out here with him on these gorgeous summer nights, when it seemed the entire sky was a billowing purple blanket made for Montana, and Montana alone.

He found the swing calming, therapeutic, even. Maybe because he was getting older. Or maybe he just appreciated the silence more than he used to. Whatever the reason, he loved being out here when the crickets chirped underneath the porch, and the occasional frog would croak in the small creek running next to his property.

But tonight, Francie sat next to him, her leg brushing his. She didn't seem to mind the silence, either. In fact, she seemed to revel in it. She had her head leaned all the way back, staring at the sky where the swirling, darkened clouds lay, and the first of the muted stars peeked through.

He looked over at her, loving her. Not wanting to love

her. Hating the fact that he'd let himself care this much, and wondering what the hell he was going to do about it.

She smiled slightly but didn't move. Just kept looking up at the sky with those pretty blue eyes.

"What?" she asked.

"You really want to know?"

"Tell me."

They kept rocking, the swing creaking comfortingly underneath them. "I'd like to take you inside and get you out of those clothes," he said. "I want you to stay the night. And tomorrow night. I want to wake up with you in my bed. And I don't really know what to do with that, Francie. Do you?"

She lifted her head from the back of the swing, and looked over then, the smile fading from her lips. There was a worry line between her brows—something new.

He reached over and smoothed it with his thumb. He didn't want to see her sad, or worried, or hurt. But that wasn't realistic, was it? Despite the act she put on for everyone else, she was a human being, not a mannequin. She was going to be imperfect, she was going to be sad and worried, because she had a beating heart.

"I want all those things, too," she said. "But I'm afraid to want them. Just like you're afraid to want them."

His gaze dropped to her mouth, soft and pink in the evening light. He thought he'd fallen for her all those years ago. Turns out, he'd never known how far a man could fall until that moment.

"I would never intentionally hurt you. You know that, right?"

She nodded.

"I don't want to screw this up," he continued. "I don't want to screw things up with Maddie." He looked out at the mountains, how they jutted toward the sky like gnarled fingers, and thought of his mom then. How she'd treated relationships like boxed chocolates. If she didn't like the taste of one, she'd simply throw it out and try another. It hadn't mattered that her boys had gotten close to some of the men she'd brought home. That she'd told them it was okay, *this* one was different. But they'd always turned out to be the same. Again and again and again.

The memory was enough to make him feel short of breath on this close to perfect night, with this close to perfect woman. Why couldn't he get past it? Why couldn't he accept that he was a grown man who was capable of making better choices? That opening himself up for once didn't mean he was weak or irresponsible, or that he would fuck up his life by letting people into it?

Francie put her hand on his thigh. "Tanner."

He didn't look at her. He was afraid if he did, something might happen to him. He felt weird, like when he was twelve and couldn't get the words past his vocal chords. When his tongue wouldn't cooperate and tangled like a rope in his mouth.

"I'm just going to say it," she said, "because I need to. Because I think you need to hear it."

He put his hand over hers. "Don't."

She stiffened.

"I love you," she finally said. "I'm in love with you, and

it doesn't matter how you feel about that right now. Even though it's kind of petrifying, I'll be honest, it's not going to change how *I* feel."

He sat rooted in place, his heart beating painfully inside his chest. He stared out at the yard that he'd worked so hard on, because he wanted to be a good home owner, a good neighbor, and by association, a responsible member of the community. Something his mother had never been. Definitely something her boyfriends had never been. He wanted a fresh start—to have a business here. A life here. So why was it so goddamn hard to believe he deserved one?

He tried moving his hand away. He didn't think about it, it was just instinctual. When things got too deep, he wanted to get as far away as possible. He understood this about himself.

But Francie held on. It was a risk, she had to know that. But still, she didn't let go.

"I know you might not love me back," she said. "And that's okay, because you probably haven't loved anyone for a really long time. But I want you to know I'm not going anywhere. Not unless you want me to. I'm not gonna just disappear on you, Tanner. I'm not going to walk away from Maddie, even if she's living all the way across the ocean. She's going to know I'm here for her, no matter what, okay?"

His skin felt tight, itchy. He wanted her to go. And he wanted her to stay. The crickets chirped and a car passed in front of the house, its headlights cutting into the dusky light. The world had never felt this small, or this big, in his entire life.

She sat there breathing hard, waiting. He'd told her he wouldn't intentionally hurt her. Was that what he'd do by simply sitting there and keeping his mouth shut? But he didn't know what to say, how to react, because he didn't trust himself. All he knew was that he wanted her. He wanted to feel her hair against his bare chest, he wanted to feel her moving underneath him. He wanted to hear those words coming from her lips again. Jesus help him, he did.

Pushing off the swing, he stood and turned to look down at her. She stared back, completely vulnerable to whatever he chose to do next. And he realized then that it wasn't leaving or staying that would make him most like his mother. It was not doing anything at all.

So he extended his hand, until she put hers into it. He helped her up and pulled her close. Her body was soft and giving, molding to his like clay. He caught her subtle perfume and he breathed her in, feeling almost drunk on her.

She wrapped her arms around his waist, and he wondered how much of what she'd just said, she'd meant. Would she stick around? But when was sticking worth it? He guessed that was the million-dollar question the kid in him still craved an answer to. When were you supposed to stay, and when were you supposed to go?

Pushing that aside, pushing everything else aside, he bent to kiss her neck. He splayed his hand across her lower back, feeling the curve of it, the absolute femininity of what made her Francie.

She tipped her head back to look up at him. Her hair brushed his arms, which made him want to wrap his hands in it. With her, there was no halfway.

Again, he let himself wonder what it would be like to have her stay, not just tonight, but every night. What it would be like to keep Maddie close, to raise her the way Luke had suggested. He let himself go there for a second, maybe two. And instead of his throat tightening the way it always did, there was a sensation of warmth, pure and sweet, that bled into his chest.

It was a first.

"Kiss me, Tanner," she said.

And he did.

Chapter Sixteen

FRANCIE STOOD AT her kitchen sink unloading the dishwasher as the morning sun shone in warm, cheerful rays through the window. It was a beautiful day—a blue, cloudless sky, a soft, summer breeze, and a full heart close to bursting. That last part didn't have anything to do with the weather, but still.

Standing on her tiptoes, she put a pair of glass mugs on the top shelf. She and Maddie had used them for root beer floats the other night. They'd painted each other's toenails and watched an episode of *Stranger Things* while Tanner worked late getting some mulch spread after the sun had gone down and the day had cooled some. He'd shown up dirty and sweaty, and honestly, the sexiest she'd probably seen him yet. And that was saying something. She'd seen him naked.

Smiling at that, she bent for some plates, but paused when the phone rang from the counter. Seeing Audrey's name flash on the screen, she reached for it.

"Hello?"

"Don't kill me."

She looked down at her bubblegum-pink toes, standing

out against the white linoleum. "Now, why would I do that?"

"You're a good person," Audrey said, the reception crackly. Francie could tell she was driving. She lived near the lake and the reception there was notoriously spotty. "And you normally wouldn't murder your best friend. But the day has come when you might consider it."

"What? What are you talking about?"

"My grandmother."

Francie groaned before she could help it. Audrey's grandma was sweet and loveable but was constantly trying to marry Audrey off. And if it wasn't Audrey, it was Francie, whom she thought was desperate by association. The stories of her failed matchmaking ventures were legendary.

"What now?"

"She ran into Guy at Rocco's the other night. He was alone. And he asked about you."

Her stomach dropped. "Oh, my God. Should I be worried?"

"Weeelll…"

"Audrey."

"She kind of told him you were unattached, which, to her credit…I *guess*…means she didn't know about Tanner."

Francie bit her top lip and stared up at the ceiling as the connection cut out, then crackled back to life. "And?"

"And…she sort of gave him your address."

"What?"

"I know. Oh, my God, I know. But you can't hurt me because I'm just the messenger."

Francie squeezed the phone and started pacing back and forth. "Agnes, Agnes, Agnes..."

"I had a talk with her. She promises never to do it again. She loves you, Fran. You know how she is."

As horrifying as it was that Guy now knew where she lived, she couldn't find it in her heart to be too annoyed. Audrey's grandma couldn't help it if she was the worst cupid ever born.

"I know," Francie said. "It's okay."

"It's really not, but now what?"

"Do you think he'll show up?" It was a rhetorical question. They both knew he would.

"Tanner thinks you still have something for Guy, doesn't he?"

"Yes."

"And your neighbor in the yellow bungalow is a huge gossip, right?"

Francie rubbed her temple. "Yup."

"Well, you just have to cut Guy off at the pass, then. Call him before he comes over and the whole town finds out, for God's sake."

"You're right. I need to call him." The thought turned her stomach. She didn't want to, but a phone call was better than seeing him in person.

The phone crackled again. "Fran, I'm gonna lose you. Call you later? You *have* to tell me what he says."

"Okay. Love you."

"Love you, too."

And the line went dead.

Francie's palms were clammy. Things with Tanner were so perfect right now, so delicate. He was just now beginning to trust her. All she needed was Guy Davis fueling that fire inside him that had been burning since childhood.

Francie looked at the clock. Almost ten. He'd be here any minute with Maddie. He'd taken her with him on an early job because she'd wanted to help plant some flowers, but they were supposed to stop by Francie's midmorning for donuts and coffee before he got going again.

She wiped her hands down the front of her shorts. She needed to call Guy *now*. Nothing said he'd show up, but nothing said he wouldn't, either. She just prayed she still had his number in her purse from when she'd seen him in town before. If not, she could track him down at his office. All of a sudden, nothing was more important than keeping him away from her and Tanner—and fiercely protecting what was growing between them. And that was new for her. Very new.

Heading into the living room, she stopped in her tracks when the doorbell chimed. Tanner and Maddie never used the doorbell. They always knocked.

She looked out the window but couldn't see a car at the curb. Maybe it was just Stephanie from next door bringing back that fan she'd borrowed last week. Or maybe it was the little girl who delivered her paper—sometimes she brought it up to the door to be sweet. There were roughly a gagillion people it could be, but Francie's stomach twisted anyway.

Padding up to the door, she took a steadying breath and opened it.

Standing there on her porch was none other than Guy

Davis. Her mouth went immediately dry. She'd been expecting this, but even for him it was fast. All she could do was blink for a second like an idiot.

He wore pressed khaki slacks and a pristine white dress shirt, open at the collar. His cologne practically knocked her over from where she stood, and she took a step back.

He smiled slowly. As if his showing up on her doorstep was a gift he'd chosen to bestow, and she should be grateful.

He held out a Styrofoam cup. "Here's that coffee we talked about. Since you were too shy, I thought I'd just bring it over."

That was just like Guy. To assume the reason she hadn't rushed out to coffee with him was because she was *shy*. Of course, she hadn't exactly told him no, either. And a little voice in the back of her head slammed her for that. *See? This is exactly what Tanner was talking about. Why can't you just tell people off?*

Before she knew it, he'd opened the screen door and stepped past, looking smug and arrogant.

She turned and gaped at him.

"Nice place," he said, glancing around.

"Guy."

"Yeah." He turned, handing her the cup of coffee.

"You need to leave."

His gaze settled on hers as if he had no idea what she was talking about. The light was on, but no one was home.

"I'm sorry?"

"I'm seeing someone," she said bluntly, holding the coffee back out to him. "And you showing up like this doesn't feel like wanting to catch up. It feels like something different, so I'm telling you now. I'm not single anymore."

Her ears were throbbing. Never in her life had she been this straightforward. Ever. She'd been taught to protect other people's feelings, even at the sake of her own. She was a polite girl. A girl who always charmed, even while letting down softly.

There was a quick flash of irritation in Guy's eyes. He was a wealthy, powerful investor. Obviously used to getting his way. He'd been like this in high school, too. He'd wanted the best, the most desirable, and Francie guessed that's what she'd been. On the surface, at least. To people like him who didn't bother to look any deeper.

"Oh, yeah?" he finally said, taking the coffee back. "And who's that?"

She didn't have to tell him. She didn't have to explain anything. But all of a sudden, the memories came rushing back like a bitter flood—Guy taunting Tanner, Guy laughing at him behind his back. Suddenly, she wanted him to know who her heart belonged to. She wanted him to know that being the most powerful didn't always mean you won in the end. Sometimes it just meant you were an asshole.

Pushing her shoulders back, she raised her chin. "Tanner Harlow."

Guy stared at her for a long, gut-wrenching moment. Then his lips stretched into a thin smile and he laughed. The sound set her teeth on edge, made her see a red so vibrant, it threatened to blind her where she stood.

"Tanner Harlow? Fran, come on. You're *dating* that

guy?"

She reached over and yanked the door open. "You bet your ass."

"Honey, I'm sorry for laughing, I am. But he's a nobody. He's always been a nobody."

Her eyes stung. She didn't think she'd ever been so livid in her life. "Excuse me?"

He stepped forward, right into her space. God, she was sick of that. His cologne was too much. It made her want to throw up.

"Remember," he said, his voice thick with animosity, "*C-c-catcher in the Rye?*"

Her eyes flew open and she froze solid, unable to believe what she'd just heard. "*What* did you just say?"

"You're trying to tell me the guy's got his shit all worked out? Just because he grew doesn't mean he can think straight. He's a fucking yard guy for Christ's sake." He shook his head. "Wow. You're really shooting for the stars."

Her hand trembled at her side. She'd never slapped anyone before. Never even considered it. But she was considering it now.

"I'm ashamed I was ever with you, Guy. The fact that I let you touch me makes me physically sick. I guess I always wanted to see the best in you in high school, but we're not kids anymore. You don't get to stand here in my house and call me honey. And you *definitely* don't get to say one word about Tanner. You don't know him, you never did. He was more of a man at fifteen than you'll ever be. Ever."

His lips hardened, as his face turned red. Then a deeper

red. Then faintly purple. For the first time, it occurred to her that maybe she wasn't safe with him in her house. She'd hit a chord. A deep, sensitive chord. For whatever reason, the comparison to Tanner enraged him.

"You never stood up for me like this, did you?" His voice was barely a whisper.

"You were never worth it."

She'd said it before she could think twice. But the truth always found its way out, even so many years later. Even when it had been buried for so long. She'd chosen to look the other way as a girl. And now she had to own that. But it wasn't too late to start again. To be the woman she'd always wanted to be, but never had the guts to embrace.

"You two deserve each other," he said softly. "The little piece of ass, and the white trash from the shitty part of town."

She stood rooted in place. She could feel his breath on her face, sour and warm. "Get out."

He smiled again, but this time there was no semblance of humor there. Only bitterness. He watched her steadily with his small eyes, a fat vein bulging in his forehead.

Francie's heart beat like a rabbit's behind her breastbone. And then, finally, he set the coffee cup down on the end table and turned to go without another word.

She watched him walk out the door and down the steps into the morning sun, his thick shoulders moving underneath his shirt like an animal's. That's what he reminded her of right then. A bull. Only acting on instinct. No warmth or empathy at all, which shouldn't have surprised her.

With shaking hands, she closed the door. And locked it for good measure.

She needed an aspirin.

Chapter Seventeen

"NO," MADDIE SAID with a laugh, leaning against the open window. "That's her old album. And there was never a song in there about him, either."

Tanner smiled, keeping his eyes on the road. The sun was bright this morning, the air buffeting his arms already warm. It was going to be hot later, and he had probably ten hours of work ahead of him. But he felt more alive than he had in a long time. The governor's assistant had called and left a message on his voicemail. They wanted him as soon as he could make room in his schedule. It'd be at least a week's job and he'd need to hire someone, which he didn't want to rush. Quaking Aspen was finally taking off, something that filled him with pride and an overwhelming sense of accomplishment. But that wasn't why he felt the way he did this morning. That had everything to do with the woman he couldn't get out of his head, no matter how hard he tried.

She was changing things for him. The way he looked at people, the way he approached life in general. He felt the outer walls around his heart beginning to crumble, and it was an experience that he found he wanted to savor. Like an expensive steak or a tall glass of porter after a long day in the sun. She had that effect. All this was so new, that sometimes he had to stop and remind himself that just a few months ago if someone had asked him what being in love felt like, he honestly wouldn't have known how to answer.

He turned his big truck onto Bramble Lane and lowered the sun visor. Neighborhood kids were out in droves this morning, sprinklers were on, and people were walking their dogs. Marietta was a good place to live. A good place to raise a family. Tanner wondered if that was in the cards for him. For Maddie. Or would she grow up in Hawaii, estranged from three brothers she'd only really known as a kid?

Pushing a hand through his hair, he narrowed his eyes at the car parked around the corner from Francie's house. Black. Something that looked fast and douchey. And vaguely familiar.

He gripped the steering wheel harder. It could be anyone. There were lots of nice cars around here. But something tickled his subconscious like a feather anyway.

Maddie was yammering on about the difference between being a Taylor Swift *fan* and a Swifty. Apparently there was enough of one that it needed explanation.

He nodded, but kept his gaze trained on the car.

And then, as he pulled up to the curb, he saw him. Guy fucking Davis. Walking down Francie's front steps, with that familiar asshole swagger.

A slow, hot pulse built at his temples as he put the truck in Park. As he reminded himself that Francie was her own woman—he didn't own her. They weren't married, and even if they were, a classmate on her doorstep didn't necessarily mean jack shit.

That's what he told himself. But deep down, he knew better. Guy being there meant nothing good. Nothing good at all.

"Who's that?" Maddie asked, looking from Tanner to Guy, and back again.

He swallowed, which wasn't easy. His tongue felt twice its normal size. "An old friend of Francie's."

"That's a nice car."

"Stay here, okay?"

"But—"

He opened the door and turned to give her a look. "Stay here, Maddie."

Normally she'd argue with that—lately she'd insisted on sticking to him like glue. But his expression must've conveyed more than he thought, because she snapped her mouth shut and sat back obediently in the seat.

Stepping out onto the street, he closed the door. Guy hadn't seen him yet, and Tanner hooked his thumbs in his pockets and walked around the front of the truck.

The other man stopped on the walkway, turned toward Francie's window, and cupped a hand around his mouth. "Thanks for the coffee, honey!"

A feeling that Tanner couldn't really identify crawled through his chest then. It wasn't anger. It wasn't quite jealously, either, although he'd be lying if he said he didn't feel a little of both. But at the forefront was a unique kind of disappointment that he'd never experienced before, and never wanted to again, if he could help it.

He knew it wasn't fair to jump to conclusions, that Francie deserved better than that. But at the same time, he wanted to take her by the shoulders and demand why in the world she'd do this. After everything he'd told her and after she'd convinced him that she'd grown. Inviting this prick into her house sure didn't seem like growth. It seemed like exactly the opposite.

Guy turned and finally saw him. There was a shocked look on his ruddy face. And then the shock settled into something else. Something Tanner recognized from their adolescence.

Tanner kept his thumbs in his pockets and leaned casually against the grill of his truck. "How's it going?"

The other man smiled thinly. "Harlow. Long time, no see."

"Yeah. Nice morning."

"Sure is." He nodded toward Tanner's truck, where Maddie sat watching. "See you finally started your own lawn-mowing business, huh?"

Tanner's shoulders tensed, and he felt a distinctive heat making its way up his neck. But he gave him an easy smile. "I leave the lawn mowing to the kid down the street. Good kid. Could teach you a thing or two about an honest day's work."

Guy clenched his jaw. Tanner could see the meaty muscles working from where he stood. They watched each other, a primitive energy crackling between them.

The other man took a step forward and pulled his keys from his pocket, jingling them obnoxiously. "I don't know that you should be lecturing me about work, Harlow. One of us has people kissing his ass on the job. The other is just a blue-collar grunt. Not knocking it, though. It's a way to pay the bills."

Fury curled inside Tanner's chest. Still, he looked down at his boots and scuffed at the cement, aware that Maddie hung on every word.

"Haven't changed much, have you, Guy? Still a total dickhead."

The other man laughed, but it was strained. "You were a pretty easy target, you have to admit."

Tanner pictured the kid he'd been, skinny, small, trying to string two sentences together without tripping over the words. In front of everyone. In front of the girl he'd adored. Nobody, unless they'd lived through it, would ever know how hard it was to be the subject of ridicule and blind contempt by someone who thought they were better, simply by being bigger.

Guy still thought he was bigger. Bigger life, more expensive car, more powerful job. He was a sorry excuse for a man, and everything Tanner wanted to protect Maddie from at that moment.

They were only a few feet away from each other now, the space between them not nearly big enough for how Tanner was feeling. Twitchy, unpredictable. He struggled to keep leaning indifferently against his truck, when all he wanted was to take the other man by the throat.

"Why don't you get in your car," Tanner said, "and go back to where you came from? You and I, we've got nothing else to say to each other."

Guy took another step forward. He was thick, but Tanner dwarfed him. It didn't matter though, because he knew Tanner would take the goddamn high road. And a man like Guy would always take advantage of that until the day he died.

"Francie's pretty sweet, isn't she?" Guy muttered, his expression mildly disgusting.

Tanner stared at him, his pulse humming in his ears.

"Almost like honey," he continued, shaking his head. "She tastes just like it."

His vision, which had been narrowing before, faded to black. He could hear his own shallow breaths, one after the other.

Guy reached out and tapped his chest. "Hey, enjoy my seconds, man."

A lightning bolt exploded behind Tanner's eyes. He grabbed the other man by the shirt and hauled him up until he balanced on the toes of his loafers.

"I'm going to break your fucking *face* if you don't get the hell out of here," Tanner said. Then let go and shoved him hard.

Guy stumbled back, his eyes wide. He stood there for a second, as if deciding whether or not to fight. Finally, he bent to pick up his keys from the cement. "Go to hell, Harlow."

"You first."

"She *wanted* me here."

Maybe. Maybe not. That was something Tanner was going to have to come to terms with later. Right now he just needed to get Maddie out of there. She'd gotten out of the truck and was standing on the sidewalk looking like she was about to cry. *Perfect.*

"Maddie, we're leaving."

"But—"

"I'm taking you home," he growled. "Get in the truck."

Biting her lip, she did as she was told.

Guy headed to his car, glancing back a few times to make sure Tanner wasn't following.

"Tanner?"

He looked up to see Francie on her front porch, staring at Guy.

"What happened?"

He didn't know how to answer that. Right then, he was still too pissed, too worked up to say much of anything. He'd let this happen. He'd let his guard down and look where it had gotten him. Right back to high school.

All he knew was that he'd managed to show Maddie nothing more than what she'd seen from every other man in her life. She'd needed him to be different. So much for taking the high road.

"I'll call you later," he said.

And climbed into his truck, forcing himself not to give her another look.

Chapter Eighteen

FRANCIE PULLED UP to Tanner's house with her heart twisting.

She'd only caught the tail end of it—Guy tripping backward, Tanner looking more furious than she'd ever seen him, and Maddie hugging herself on the sidewalk. *God.*

Parking the car, she glanced at the house. He hadn't answered his phone when she'd called on the way over. And the way he'd looked when he'd driven off... His expression had left her cold and a little scared. She'd thought about him holding her the other night after she'd told him she loved him. He hadn't said it back. And that was okay. It was. She could live with that for a while, because right now she could love him enough for the both of them. But what she couldn't live with would be his shutting her out.

She pulled in a deep breath and got out of the car, closing the door behind her. She walked up the steps with her pulse tapping behind her ear, then stood outside his door, gathering herself. The morning had gotten hot, and she felt a trickle of sweat between her breasts. Her hair was heavy on the back of her neck, and for the first time in her life, she pictured cutting it. Her mother would have a coronary. But maybe it was time Loretta Tate started learning to accept a few things about her daughter. Like whom she loved and wanted to be with.

Finally, she raised her fist and knocked. From inside Charlotte barked a few times, but then fell silent. There were no footsteps headed toward the door, no shout from inside that he'd be right there.

She waited, forcing herself to keep breathing. He was definitely home. His truck was parked out front. He took Charlotte everywhere with him. Which meant, he didn't want to see her.

She stared at the door, her instincts screaming at her to leave. To protect herself from this pain while she still could. Tanner was more intricate than any man she'd ever been with. He was like a painting that you stared at, trying to understand the choice behind the brush strokes. Deep down, she knew that standing her ground meant the possibility of rejection. That's what she feared the most. And the deeper in love she fell, the more real that fear became.

She recognized right then that he was going to do his best to push her away. Maybe because he didn't trust her. Maybe because he was terrified of being anything other than numb. Or maybe just because Tanner Harlow, the man who towered over her, was really just the same little boy he'd been all those years ago. Because he'd never come to terms with his parents, with his own pain, enough to negotiate his life without being defensive as a stone wall.

Licking her lips, she squared her shoulders. She didn't feel big enough to take him on. She didn't feel strong enough. But she was going to try. And if he broke her into a thousand little pieces in the process, then so be it. At least she'd know for once in her life that she stood up for something real.

She raised her fist and knocked again. This time, harder.

And this time she heard footsteps coming from inside. Heavy, purposeful.

The door opened, and there he was. Handsome, and as dark as an impending summer storm. He didn't smile, just stood there looking down at her with his jaw working.

Her heart pounded from nerves, lust, longing, fear. Anything and everything all wrapped together in a tidy little bow. She swallowed hard, forcing herself to look right back.

"You weren't going to answer the door?"

He watched her, as if deciding how to answer that. Then shrugged in the most infuriating way. "Maybe."

She crossed her arms over her chest. "Are you going to let me in?"

"I'm kind of busy. Have to get back to work."

"Tanner."

"What?"

"We need to talk."

"I don't know that I want to talk."

She glared up at him. "Okay. So we're going to pretend you didn't just have it out with Guy on my walkway?"

"Was that your walkway? Hadn't noticed."

"Now you're being ridiculous."

His jaw bunched.

"You obviously think I invited him over," she said.

"Did you?"

"Of course not."

"But you had coffee."

"He *brought* coffee. There's a difference."

"Okay. He brought coffee. But you invited him in."

She hesitated at that. She hadn't invited him in, but she *had* let him in. She chewed the inside of her cheek for a long second. "I can't stand Guy," she finally said. "I didn't want to be in the same room with him."

"Then why *were* you, Francie?" His eyes flashed. "You knew what he came there for." He was frustrated, angry. And for the first time she saw that he was genuinely confused, too. He wanted an answer to the question she'd been asking herself for years. *Why do you have to be so damn pleasing all the time?*

Her throat ached. "Honestly?"

"Yeah. Honestly."

"It was out of habit." And there it was. It was as simple as that. As disappointing as that. "I wish I had a different explanation for you, Tanner. I wish I had a different one for me, too. But that's the truth."

He stared down at her, his face a blank canvas.

"Don't you see?" She hated the sound of her voice, the sound of pleading. But she wanted him to understand. *Needed* him to understand who she was deep down. Because if he didn't, who would? "I've never rocked the boat," she managed. "I've never made anyone uncomfortable, or angry. That's why I stayed with Guy so long in high school. That's why I entered all those pageants for my mom. Why I have friends who still think they can walk all over me."

His expression softened a little at that, but she felt her back stiffen. She didn't want his sympathy. She wanted him to believe in her.

"It's why I let him in today, even though I clearly shouldn't have. But you know what?"

His brows rose.

"I'm glad I did," she continued. "Because today was different. I finally broke that cycle. I told him off and it was actually...pretty great."

Warmth flooded her cheeks. She was proud of herself, and that was the puzzle piece that had been missing her entire life.

His lips tilted. "You did?"

She nodded.

"Damn. I wish I could've been there to see that."

"You almost were."

His gaze traveled over her hair, her mouth, then finally settled on her eyes. "You've always been stronger than you thought, Francie," he said. "It was just a matter of time before you figured it out. At least Guy has one redeeming quality—he helped you find your way."

She took a step forward, longing for him to touch her. To kiss her. "He didn't help me find anything. You did that."

He laughed, but it was bitter sounding. "Yeah."

"Why is that so hard for you to believe?"

At that, he turned and walked inside the house. She followed and shut the door behind her. Charlotte trotted up for a pat, but Maddie was nowhere in sight.

"It's so quiet in here," she said.

"She's riding her bike. I told her I needed a little time. She did, too. I'll have to figure out how to explain this when she comes back."

Francie frowned, watching him. "What happened, Tanner?"

He pinched the bridge of his nose. His biceps bulged tantalizingly, the veins sticking out on his forearms—something that sent hot, electric currents through her body.

"This was a bad idea from the beginning," he said. "And I own that. I couldn't keep my hands off you, and that was all me."

Heat crept up her face. Her eyes stung. He was going to try and hurt her, but she'd been expecting this. He was trying to push her away.

"I didn't exactly keep my hands off *you*," she said, raising her chin. "You don't get to take all the credit. We're in this together, remember?"

He turned and began pacing the floor. His sheer size was intimidating. So was his body language. It was as though every muscle in his body was coiled.

"I needed to keep my head on straight for Maddie," he said. "I needed to be someone solid for her. Who the hell almost decks someone right in front of their little sister? She was right behind me, for Christ's sake."

"I'm guessing he deserved it."

"Doesn't matter. I should've shown her how to rise above it. Just once, just *once*, she could've had a decent example. Instead, she cried all the way home."

Francie's heart ached at that. She stepped closer but he stepped back.

"I could tell you about all the things she saw my mom's boyfriends do, but I won't. The list is too long."

"Tanner, you *aren't* one of those guys," she said. "You're her brother who loves her. Maybe you made a mistake, but she knows you're different. You'll find a way to explain so she understands."

He stopped pacing and turned to her, lacing his hands above his head. "I wanted this time with her to count."

"It *has* counted. Are you kidding me? She adores you."

Dropping his arms to his sides, he stared out the window. "I don't think I could do this full-time. I'd go out of my goddamn mind trying not to screw her up."

"Well, you're just going to have to get over that."

He looked over, his gaze settling on hers.

"Maddie needs *you*," she continued softly. "She doesn't need you to be perfect. She just needs you in her life. And just because you did something you wish you hadn't, doesn't mean you couldn't raise her, Tanner. It doesn't mean she's going to be some kind of deviant now. This is what being a dad is. It's making mistakes and rectifying them. Reminding yourself to be better next time."

He opened his mouth, but she held up her hand.

"And who's to say she didn't learn something incredible today?" she asked. "Personally, *I* think turning the tables on Guy was pretty awesome."

His lips curved slightly. And some of the darkness in his

expression receded.

She wanted to go to him if he'd have her. Let him do exactly what he wanted, even if it meant risking pain in the long run. But she forced herself to stand still. She needed to know something first. She needed to know she meant something to him. Even if it wasn't love. It had to be something other than lust.

"But why?" she asked. "Why did you confront him?"

He watched her for what seemed like forever. The room had gone quiet. The air conditioning had kicked off, and Charlotte had retreated into the back room. It was just the two of them, standing there looking at each other. She thought of how often they'd done this in just a matter of weeks—this dancing around how they really felt, trying to reconcile it so they could move on.

But things always seemed to lead right back to this showdown of wills. With him trying to bury his past, and her trying to prove herself. Would it ever get any easier?

Finally, he took a step toward her. She waited, as agonizing as that was. She wanted to know exactly what he'd say. If he'd say anything at all.

Slowly, he reached out and ran the backs of his knuckles down her bare arm. His skin was so warm, so rough, that it left chills over hers.

She prayed for the strength to stand her ground. He smelled so good, so *male*. She knew exactly how her nipples would feel rubbing against his naked chest, how they'd tingle and send shock waves through the rest of her. She knew how his mouth would feel traveling down her neck, how his lips would play at the base of her throat. Still, she stayed as still as her body would allow, and watched him like a lamb contemplating a lion.

"He said you tasted like honey," Tanner said, his voice gravelly. "And Jesus help me, I couldn't stand the thought of him touching you."

Her heart pounded in her chest, her pulse skipping in her wrists. He leaned down close enough that she felt the warmth of his breath against her cheek.

"You're too good for him, Francie. You're too good for me."

At that, she finally reached up and wrapped her arms around his neck. Then stood on her tiptoes and kissed him.

He immediately opened his mouth, coaxing her closer, deeper with his tongue. She leaned into the solidness of his body. Nothing could reach her there. Not the world, not insecurity, not regret. Nothing. It was just the two of them in the moment, falling toward one another as they seemed destined to do.

Still kissing her, he pushed her toward the hallway bathroom.

She felt him hard against her lower belly, and she reached down to rub him there. Breaking the kiss, he groaned against her neck.

They stumbled toward the door, then pushed inside, their hands all over each other. Desperate and hungry.

Francie unbuckled his belt as he put his hands in her hair. He bent to kiss her again and she felt the breath being stolen from her chest. Every last bit of it. She couldn't get enough of him—his scent, his voice, the feel of him.

She was vaguely aware of him opening the medicine cabinet and pulling out a condom. He turned her around and placed her hands on the wall.

"Don't move," he said into her ear.

She closed her eyes, wanting desperately to turn back around, to feel every hot, throbbing inch of him. But she did as she was told, and the sensation of wanting to touch him, but not being able to, was almost too much to bear.

He moved her hair off the back of her neck, and then she felt his lips there. She moaned softly and in response, he pushed himself against her. She spread her legs and arched her back, and she heard him unwrap the foil packet. And then he was working her shorts down over her thighs, then her panties, until she finally felt him nudge her slick, wet opening.

She sucked in a breath, her heart nearly pounding out of her chest. He reached underneath her T-shirt and cupped her breast over her lacy bra. She longed for him to get her naked, wanted him to pick her up as he had all those weeks ago and carry her straight to his bed. But what they were doing was risky enough with Maddie right down the street. It'd have to be fast, primal. And Francie was okay with that, too. He made primal and fast an art form.

Holding her steady and safe, he slipped inside her darkness. She exhaled softly as they began moving together, creating a rhythm that was like the sweetest music—only she could feel it throughout her entire body. Thumping in her ears, her veins, her head. *Love, love, love,* it seemed to say, until the strength of her mounting orgasm took over, and everything lit up behind her eyes.

He breathed against her neck, said her name, held her so close that she could feel his heart beating against her shoulder blades.

And it pounded in sync with her own.

Chapter Nineteen

TANNER KNELT BESIDE Maddie, the sun hot on his back. His little sister was elbow-deep in mulch and had a smear of dirt across her nose. Her ponytail was limp and the fine hair at her temples was damp, but she'd insisted on coming with him to his last job of the day.

They were planting a sequoia for Bob Newhouse, his friend who worked the front desk of the Graff, Marietta's oldest and stateliest hotel. Bob firmly believed more was *always* better, thus the baby tree that would eventually grow into a giant to dwarf his entire house. Bob didn't care. In fact, Tanner was sure that five years from now, he'd enlist the local fire department to string Christmas lights all the way to the top.

Maddie wiped her hands on her jeans and looked over at him through her smudged glasses. They hadn't talked since that morning. Since he'd almost punched the living shit out of Guy.

She'd walked in the door five minutes after Francie had gone home. She'd been quiet and broody, so he'd left it alone, knowing he'd broach it when the time was right.

Here, now, kneeling with her in the middle of Bob's yard

that reminded him of a Disney movie with all the ivy and roses, he took a deep breath, hoping he wouldn't mess it up.

"Maddie," he began, "I know—"

"Do you love Francie?"

He stared at her. His mom used to do that—pop questions that would leave him stunned. He could see some of her in Maddie now. Unexpected will and stubbornness, which had a way of unnerving people.

"I…"

"Because I feel like if you love someone, you should never let them go. No matter what."

He watched her, and she watched him back, her big hazel eyes sharp. She wasn't going to settle for any bullshit answer. Maybe a year ago. But not now. She'd grown up a little over the summer. Some of that tender innocence was gone, in its place a shrewdness that he knew would serve her well later in life. Still though, he was sad to see her change at all. He wondered how different she'd be after six months of being in Hawaii—after being with Vivian and Rob.

He breathed in the smell of freshly cut grass, of cool dirt, and Maddie's scent—something fruity and clean. And then looked over at the tree that waited to be lowered into the ground so it could spread its roots, find its home.

"I do love her," he said quietly. "But it's complicated."

Maddie sighed. Like she was tired of explaining things to adults. "I don't see what's complicated about loving someone. If I loved someone, I'd want to be with them. Even if it was hard. Even if I didn't know how to do it right, I'd still try."

His gaze settled on her again. "I love you, too, Mads."

She waved a bee away from her face.

"I know you want to stay here," he continued. "But that's complicated, too."

"Only a few more weeks. Only a few more weeks, and then I'll have to go. And I won't see you and Luke and Judd. I won't see Francie, either. She'll forget about me." Her eyes welled with angry tears. "I don't *want* to go."

He reached for her, but she leaned away. The bee buzzed around her ear again, probably attracted by the smell of her shampoo. Maddie batted at it.

"I know you don't," he said. "And I don't want you to."

"Then *why* can't I stay here? Why can't we be a family?"

The words tore at his conscience. She could stay. He could raise her. His brothers would help. But then there was the doubt—the constant doubt that wouldn't subside. He had one shot at this. Trying it and failing would have lasting effects on her that neither of them would be able to comprehend for years to come. This was too important to fuck up. It was his job not to cave, even if Maddie didn't understand why.

Still, he was more tempted than he'd ever been to reach out and pull her into a hug. He wanted to tell her he wasn't going to let her go, that nothing would come between them, because they were family. They were blood.

The bee continued buzzing around Maddie's face, and she swatted at it impatiently. She stood up and brushed the dirt from her knees. "You're always saying you want what's best for me, but you don't understand how I *feel*. You're not listening to me! You're just going to send me away without understanding my side."

"I know how you feel."

"No, you don't. If you really did, you wouldn't do this." Tears welled in her eyes, then spilled down her flushed cheeks.

"What do you want from me, Maddie? I'm doing the best I can."

"You're not! You're afraid. I know you want me to stay, too. I know it! I'd be good, Tanner. I'd get good grades and I'd help with Charlotte, and I'd always keep my room clean and neat."

She was sobbing now, her glasses teetering on the edge of her nose. She was killing him dead.

The bee landed on her arm and she flinched, slapping at it again. This time she must've made contact, because after a second she yelped in pain.

He stood up and grabbed her hand, pulling her close so he could see. "Did it get you?"

She stared down at the red spot that was growing puffy before their eyes. "*Ouch.*"

Tanner grabbed his water bottle and poured some on the sting. "I'll go inside and ask Bob for some ice."

"I don't want any ice! I don't want to try and understand when I get older. I don't want to leave Marietta. I like it here." Her breath hitched in her throat. "Please don't send me away, Tanner. I love you. I want to stay *here.*"

She was practically hysterical. He took her by the shoulders and forced her to look at him. "Calm down."

"I don't want to calm down!"

She was breathing in short little pants, a faint wheeze coming from her chest.

"Maddie?"

Blinking heavily, she looked up at him. "I don't feel good."

He grabbed her arm and looked at it again. There were angry red hives all the way up it and was now so swollen that her skin was stretched taut.

"You're allergic to bees, Maddie?"

Her face had gone pale, devoid of all color. Even the sunburn she'd gotten a few days ago had all but disappeared, leaving only a spattering of freckles across her nose. And then she stumbled backward and he caught her before she went down.

With his heart in his throat, he scooped her up and ran to the truck. The hospital was only a few blocks away.

"Hang on, Mads," he said into her hair, her head flopping against his chest. "Everything's gonna be okay."

He was running under water. Everything was blurry and cold. Maddie was a toddler again, and he was holding her tight as their mother and her boyfriend fought violently in the next room. She'd sucked her thumb until she was four. He'd forgotten about that. Completely forgotten until that very second.

He yanked the driver's side door open with every muscle in his body screaming to move faster. She wasn't four anymore. She was twelve. Growing up, but still a little girl. She barely weighed anything at all. Her spindly legs bounced against his thighs, one arm hanging limply at her side. He needed to get her to eat more. He'd start making more hamburgers, her favorite. She loved hamburgers. Hamburgers, and animals, and Taylor Swift, and anything purple.

"I'm not going to let anything happen to you, Maddie," he said, choking on the words. "I promise."

⫸⫷

TANNER SAT IN one of the pleather emergency room chairs and stared up at the muted TV. *The Price Is Right* was playing on repeat. Francie sat next to him, her hand on his thigh, watching him like he was a bomb about to go off.

Which, hell. Maybe he was. So many things kept running through his mind. How had he not known she was allergic to bees? Surely she'd been stung before? And if she had, how had his mom not mentioned that?

Leaning forward, he scrubbed his face with both hands.

Francie rubbed his back. "She's going to be okay, Tanner. You got her here in plenty of time."

That's what Doctor Davidson had said when she'd come out half an hour before. She was a nice lady—a pretty redhead with a kind smile. *She's very lucky,* she'd said. *She'll be back to herself in no time, and at least now you know.*

They'd given her a shot of epinephrine, followed by a round of antihistamines and steroids. They were going to watch her for a while, and then she could go home. She was going to be tired from the trauma, the doctor said. But otherwise just fine.

He looked over at Francie, loving her for being there. He didn't want to love her for being there. He didn't want to depend on her for anything. And he *really* didn't want to feel the way he felt, as if looking at her one more second might bring him to his knees.

"What?" she asked.

He took a deep breath, putting his hand over hers. Feeling her delicate skin slide over her knuckles. The truth was, he was sick of denying things for the sake of denying them. It was that simple. Where Francie was concerned, he was so far gone, he couldn't even see straight anymore. Now he had to figure out what the hell he was going to do about it.

"Vivian knows," he said quietly.

"What?"

"I put her name down as an emergency contact, and they must've called for an insurance question or something, because she left a voicemail about ten minutes ago."

"Oh, God."

It was an accident. But they both knew Tanner blamed himself. And Vivian probably would, too. That's just how it was.

"It's okay. She'll be in charge soon. She needed to know anyway."

Francie swallowed visibly, and there was a vague look of disappointment on her face. He'd told her what happened before Maddie had been stung. How upset she'd been. How she hadn't even let him explain about Guy.

"So, you're sending her, then?"

He had to admit, he'd been wavering. After talking to

Luke, after hearing the desperation in Maddie's voice that afternoon. He was torn now—torn between feeling like he should do what was right by her, and what his heart said was right by the both of them.

"I don't know." He shook his head. "I really don't."

Chapter Twenty

TANNER HELD THE phone to his ear, looking out the window to the giant fireball of a sun which was setting in the west. He couldn't help but think of that night almost two months ago now. A night just like this one, when he found out his mother had died, and he'd be the temporary guardian of his little sister.

The grief had eased some, it wasn't as sharp as it had been. It was more of a dull ache now, deep inside his bones. He felt it, throbbing with the intensity only death and loss could bring.

"For God's sake, Tanner. She could've died." His aunt was pissed.

He'd been expecting the accusation, the presumption he didn't know what he was doing, but that didn't make it any easier to swallow.

Shifting on his feet, he reminded himself this was about Maddie, not him. She *could've* died. Vivian was absolutely right. And now there'd need to be a reckoning of sorts—she'd tell him exactly what he'd done wrong, and he'd accept it because he already felt like shit.

"I know," he said.

"How could you have not known she was allergic? Even I knew and I live three thousand miles away."

"Mom never told me."

"Mmm. Or maybe you weren't paying attention?"

He bristled at that.

"Look, Tanner." She sighed. "I'm not blaming you, honey."

"Uh-huh."

"God knows Jennifer had a habit of failing you. I'm only worried you've got too much on your plate with this guardianship. I mean, you're taking her to work with you. Why are you even doing that?"

"We were planting a tree. She wanted to come. I've got a place for her to be, but she wanted to come. It's not like I took her to a strip club with me."

"Do you...*go* to strip clubs?"

"Jesus Christ."

"I'm just asking."

He rubbed his temple. "No, Vivian. I don't go to strip clubs. Not that it'd make me inept if I did."

"It'd make you distracted. And a bad example."

"Isn't that what you think I am now?" The words were surprisingly hard to say. They struck a chord, since that was exactly what he feared he was to Maddie.

"I think you've just got too much on your plate. Like I said."

His aunt was the quintessential diplomat. She was walking a delicate wire, trying not to offend her nephew, while getting what she ultimately wanted in the end: her niece.

He stared out the window as Charlotte yawned from the couch. He looked over. She wasn't supposed to be up there, but Francie and Maddie always let her up when he wasn't looking. Something he used to mind, but now he found…sweet. That's what these two had done over the course of one summer. Changed him so slowly, he'd barely realized it, until moments like these. When he looked over at his dog on the couch and found himself a nostalgic fucking mess.

The question was, how much would he allow himself to be changed? At what point did it become too reckless? He didn't know if he had the answer to that. And if he did, he didn't know if he'd take it at face value, anyway. Maybe, just maybe, opening himself up to that recklessness didn't make him weak like he'd always thought. Maybe it meant he was stronger for taking the chance.

"Hello?" his aunt said.

"I'm here."

"I think I should go ahead and come get Maddie," she said. "Rob and I are ready, and it might make things easier in the long run. You know, so she doesn't get any more attached."

He shoved his hand in his pocket. "I'm her brother. I don't think there's anything wrong with being attached."

"Of course not. I just mean it might make the transition easier, that's all. I know you boys will be visiting a lot. You're always welcome here."

"And she'll come back to Marietta. For the summers."

"Right, right. For the summers."

He had a feeling she wanted to wrap it up. Have him say yes and hang up before he changed his mind. She didn't have to worry. He'd already made it up on the way home from the hospital. He wanted Maddie to stay. But he knew sending her would be the most responsible thing.

Even though it hurt like hell.

Chapter Twenty-One

FRANCIE STOOD IN the doorway of Maddie's room, trying to swallow down the gigantic lump in her throat. But there was no use, it wouldn't budge.

She watched the little girl reach for a plastic tote bag, and shove a stuffed hippo inside, then a few books, dog-eared and obviously loved.

Maddie looked up, tears streaking her face. "I think that's everything."

"Honey, you know you'll be back, right?" Francie said. "It'll be next summer before you know it."

"Colton will forget about me."

"Not if he's a good friend, he won't. And he's definitely a good friend."

"You'll get busy with other things. Everyone always says they'll keep in touch, but they never do."

Francie walked over to Maddie's bed and sat down beside her. "Hey. There's something you don't know about me."

Maddie brushed her knuckles underneath her chin where the tears had been dripping onto her tank top. "What?"

"I had a pen pal in the fifth grade."

The little girl sniffed.

"Yup," Francie continued. "Ava O'Rourke. We met at a beauty pageant. Little Miss Montana. Have you ever heard of it?"

Maddie laughed and shook her head.

"Yeah, well, I was a regular at those things. It was my last year and Ava's first. She was scared to death. I mean, *shaking* from head to toe. She was going to recite a poem as her talent, and backstage she was having trouble remembering the lines, so I helped her. She reminded me of someone else, someone close to you, who also recited something important to him in front of our class, even though he had a lot of trouble doing it."

Maddie watched her. "Tanner?"

Francie nodded. "She was nervous, like him. But she was also strong. Like him, too. The other girls were laughing behind her back, but the more they laughed, the more Ava recited her lines. Over and over and over. Even though she could barely stand up straight. Even though everyone thought she'd probably pass out on stage."

"What happened?"

"She didn't pass out. It wasn't easy, but she got through it. And you know what?"

"What?"

"She won the pageant."

Maddie grinned.

"Yup," Francie continued. "She won and we exchanged addresses, and the rest is history."

"Do you still write?"

Francie put an arm around her. "We do better than that. She came to visit last Christmas. She lives far away now. Canada, but she's one of my best friends in the whole world. And it all started with writing letters."

Maddie leaned against Francie's shoulder. "So you'll write?"

"And I'll call and FaceTime, too. And you'll be back to see Tanner before you know it."

At that, the little girl stiffened.

"Don't be mad at him, Maddie," Francie said. "He's only doing what he thinks is best."

"Without caring what I want."

"It goes deeper than that. I know you're tired of hearing that, but it's true."

She nodded miserably. "I know. But I don't think I can forgive him yet. I just feel so...*sad*."

Francie pulled her close. It was so hard seeing her go through this. It was confusing and difficult for her to understand. But Francie's heart also broke for Tanner, who didn't want to send her away. She knew the bee sting had acted as a nail in the coffin, and the doubts he'd had before, were now multiplied tenfold. And his aunt hadn't helped.

She and Tanner were sitting awkwardly in the living room now, waiting to take Maddie to the airport. Tanner had asked Francie if she'd wanted to come, but she had a 100 percent history of bawling during airport goodbyes, so she'd opted not to.

Even now, though, she was having a hard time composing herself. God, she was going to miss this kid. And not just

Maddie. Maddie and Tanner together, coming over to her house, playing games, watching movies, taking walks. Sometime over the past few weeks, they'd become a quirky little family. Nothing that anyone else would recognize necessarily, but she did. And she loved the three of them together with her whole heart.

There was a knock on the door, and they both looked up to see Tanner standing there.

He wore dark blue Levi's today and a gray striped polo. He looked good enough to eat. But his mood was heavy, and his lips were drawn into a thin line, reminding her how much this weighed on him.

"We'd better go if we want to get you through security in time." His gaze settled on Francie. "You sure you don't want to come?"

She nodded, not trusting herself to speak. In fact, she really needed to leave before the waterworks started in earnest.

Turning to Maddie, she gave her one more squeeze. "Text me when you get there? I can't wait to see all the beach pictures. You're gonna love it, kiddo."

Maddie hugged her back. "I'll miss you," she mumbled.

Francie leaned close and whispered in her ear, so only she could hear. "He loves you more than anything. Don't forget that, okay?"

TANNER STOOD WITH his hands in his pockets as they

waited in line. After Maddie and Vivian got to the metal detector, he wouldn't be able to go any farther. He'd have to say goodbye there.

He glanced over at his little sister who didn't look back. She just continued staring straight ahead while Vivian went on about her favorite Mexican food restaurant, which was right down the street from their house.

Vivian didn't seem offended at the lack of interest on Maddie's part. In fact, she seemed completely oblivious. She'd made a plan which made sense, and now she was executing that plan with complete precision. Like a surgeon. Clean and neat.

He didn't think he'd ever seen Maddie like this. Even after their mom had died, there'd been moments of life behind her eyes. Now, those eyes were dull and empty. Almost colorless.

She'd refused to speak to him all day, and he knew she felt betrayed. She'd said as much. *If you love someone, you should never let them go.* To her, this was just another let-down in a long line of them.

The thought was enough to make him feel like he was choking where he stood. *She'll understand when she gets older...* That's what he kept telling himself. But he wanted her to understand now. He didn't want her to get on that plane without some kind of window into his head. Into himself as her brother, and as a man.

The line moved up a few people, and Vivian busied herself digging around in her carry-on. Turning, he took Maddie by the shoulders and forced her to face him.

She gazed up from a ghostly-white face. Even her freckles didn't want to make the effort of standing out. Frowning, she waited for whatever he was going to say, and right then she seemed much older than a middle schooler.

"You know what I just remembered the other day?" he said.

She blinked up at him, her eyes glassy. She didn't answer.

"I remembered you sucked your thumb until you were four." He leaned closer, until his face was only inches from hers. "You sucked your right thumb, and that's why you learned to use a fork with your left hand."

She swallowed, watching him.

"Nobody else knows that about you, Maddie. I don't even think Luke and Judd know."

"I don't remember," she said.

"I know you don't. It's my job to remember for you."

The line moved up another few people, and Vivian stood aside, giving them some privacy. There was the roar of a jet taking off on the runway, and the muffled sound of a little boy crying into his mother's shirt sleeve a few yards away.

"I love you more than anything in the whole world," he said, struggling to keep his voice from cracking. "More than myself. I know you're mad right now. But I want you to remember that, okay? No matter what."

Tears filled her eyes. She clutched her backpack straps with both hands, and he saw her knuckles were white.

"Are you scared to fly?" he asked. It was so stupid he hadn't thought to ask before. She'd never flown except in

Judd's twin-engine Cessna, and that wasn't even close to the same thing.

She shook her head, but he could tell she wasn't going to admit if she was. She was angry, confused, hurt. She'd get on that plane without admitting a damn thing. She was stubborn as a mule.

He pulled her into a hug and dropped a kiss on top of her head. She remained stiff as a board, and he felt her warm tears soak through the front of his shirt.

"Next?" The security officer motioned them forward.

Vivian reached up to cup Tanner's cheek. He was surprised to see she was tearing up, too. Maybe she just didn't like goodbyes. Jesus, did anyone?

"We're going to take good care of her," she said. "I'll call you the second we touch down."

"Next, please," the security officer repeated patiently.

Tanner looked down at Maddie again, this time through blurry eyes. He hadn't cried when his dad left. He hadn't cried during all those days of hell in high school. He hadn't cried when his mother had died. But now, the sadness seemed to have caught up. The irony wasn't lost on him—you could grow up and run away from the pain, but you couldn't hide from it. It'd always find you.

"I love you, Mads," he said.

She stared up at him, and without another word, let Vivian pull her gently through security.

Tanner stood still as a slab of granite, watching her put her Hello Kitty backpack on the conveyer belt and take off her beat-up Converse All Stars.

She turned around after going through the metal detector, but there were too many people to see clearly. She didn't wave, didn't blow him a kiss. Just watched him over her shoulder until she and Vivian had turned a corner and were out of sight.

Chapter Twenty-Two

B ALANCING ON THE step stool, Francie reached up and stapled the last of the cardboard cutout apples above the chalkboard. She stepped back down, looking around her classroom with a critical eye. Cute, cheerful. Ready for the bombardment of third graders who'd descend on Marietta Elementary next week.

She took a deep breath, glad the décor didn't match her mood. Unless, of course, she wanted a bunch of depressed nine-year-olds trying to learn reading and math, which she didn't.

Maddie had been gone for three weeks, and Francie hadn't talked to Tanner in nearly that long. After he'd put his little sister on the plane, he'd grown withdrawn and quiet. He'd finished her front yard and immediately packed his bags for Helena and the job at the governor's house. He'd called a few times, and always sounded a million miles away. Turns out, vulnerability and Tanner Harlow didn't mix very well. Never had. It was as though Maddie had been a catalyst for everything in his life that could affect his heart, and he'd shut it down before anything else could get through. Including her.

She chewed the inside of her cheek, looking over at her phone for the fifth time that hour, as if it would magically start ringing, and it'd be him. Ready to settle into a relationship, ready to put his demons to rest once and for all.

Instead, it stayed dark and silent like the traitor it was.

The intercom buzzed and she startled.

"Fran?" It was Sheila, the receptionist. "You've got a visitor."

"Oh, yeah?"

"Audrey. She's got coffee."

Poor Audrey had been trying to cheer her up for days. The least she could do was plaster on a smile and be grateful for the caffeine.

"Thanks, Sheila. You can send her on back."

After a minute, Audrey poked her head in. "You decent?"

"I'm always decent. You know that."

Her friend sauntered in and handed her a mocha that smelled heavenly. Francie wrapped her hands around it and actually felt a little better.

"You *are* always decent, Francie," Audrey said, sitting down on a flimsy plastic chair. Her legs were so long in her skinny jeans, she looked comical. Like Bambi trying to get situated. "But I know one person who doesn't think you're so nice anymore."

She took a sip of the coffee and winced, burning her tongue. "Who's that?"

"Guy. Saw him a few days ago, and he didn't ask about you once."

"Thank God."

"His ego was a little bruised, if I'm not mistaken."

"Good. Maybe it'll wither up and die."

Audrey laughed. "Tanner should be given a medal on behalf of everyone who went to Marietta High."

"Well, I'd tell him. But he'll barely speak to me."

"He'll come around, Fran. He probably just needs some time. A lot of things happened to him this summer."

She rubbed her thumb along the paper cup and nodded. That was true. But the problem was, she didn't know if he'd actually come around. Maybe he wasn't ready to take that step. Maybe he'd never be ready. The thought broke her heart. But eventually, she was going to have to accept it and move on.

"I just didn't expect to fall so hard, so fast," Francie said. She couldn't look at Audrey right then. She was afraid if she did, she'd start crying, and she'd done enough of that to last a lifetime.

"I know you didn't. But that's how you know you got a good one, right?"

"True." She paused, thoughtful. "I think I'm the first person outside of his family that he's let himself care about for a while."

"You're probably right."

"And it's scary."

"Right again."

"But the question is, how long do I give him? How long do I allow myself to keep feeling this way?"

Audrey picked at a peeling smiley face sticker on her chair. "That's a good question. All I can tell you is, I don't think loving you back is the problem. I think it's more than that."

"I think it is, too."

"So maybe you give him as long as you can, and then, if you have to, you walk away with your heart still intact. Or, at least somewhat intact."

She looked out the window to where the leaves would be changing soon. Where there was green now, there'd be golds and oranges and deep burgundies. Marietta would come alive with color.

"How about Maddie?" Audrey asked. "How's she?"

At the mention of her name, Francie's arms felt heavy. "She's really homesick. She likes Hawaii, but she wants to come home. Montana is all she's ever known. She misses Tanner and Charlotte."

"So you're talking, then?"

"Almost every other day." She frowned. "She's sent Tanner pictures, but she hasn't called him yet. I knew she was going to struggle with this, and so did he. But I don't think anyone knew how much."

"Poor baby."

"What kills me the most is that I'm starting to hear some resignation in the things she says. She's had to grow up a lot these past few weeks. I think she's getting close to finding some peace with it and forgiving him. I'm just sorry she couldn't stay here. That it didn't work out."

Audrey stared up at her. "For all of you."

Francie smiled, and it felt wistful. "Yeah. For all of us."

TANNER SAT BACK against the trunk of the big ponderosa pine that stood looking over the governor's large, brick home. The day was hot, but not nearly as hot as the one before. Summer was almost over, and fall would be there before he knew it.

He took a long, cool swig from his water bottle, and wiped his mouth with the back of his hand. The job was going well so far, and everyone seemed happy with the results. The guy he'd hired, whose name was Alex, was a hard worker. Quiet and insightful, and good with his hands. Tanner liked him a lot.

He liked Helena, too. The views were spectacular, and so was the elaborate Victorian architecture. He'd been here before—it had a regional airport that Judd sometimes flew in and out of, but this was the first time he'd really taken the time to explore and soak it in.

After getting a bite to eat in the evenings, he'd walk around town, stopping in the stores to talk to the locals who were friendly and welcoming. But as much as he could appreciate a place like this for its beauty and opportunities, he missed Marietta and everything it had come to represent over the last year. It was his home. And as cheesy as it sounded, was where his heart was.

The past few months with Maddie and Francie had been so sweet. They'd grown into the unlikeliest of families, and he missed them both with a deep and painful ache that had moved its way into his very being. He spent his days on the sprawling emerald grounds of the governor's house, working in the sun, sweating, and thinking. He spent the nights unable to sleep, finding himself walking underneath the starry sky, just to quiet his mind a little.

He shifted now underneath the shade of the tree and looked down over the vast Helena Valley. He'd finally accepted that no amount of working or walking, or *anything* for that matter, would ease the restlessness that was now a part of his daily existence. Or at least had been since the day Maddie had gotten on that damn plane.

He'd distanced himself from Francie that day, too, recognizing it for what it was—a survival mechanism. He'd needed this time to think, to try and figure out if being alone meant being free of pain. And ironically, it was turning out to mean just the opposite. He was so in love, that being away from her felt like he was missing a vital part of himself.

Alex waved from across the south yard and took off his hat to wipe his brow. "I'm gonna break for lunch, Boss. Back in a few."

"Take your time, man," Tanner called back. "We'll start on that river rock this afternoon."

The other man nodded and headed down the sloping drive.

Tanner watched him go, until he'd disappeared behind a grove of aspen, leaving only the trees and the silence, and the steady thudding of Tanner's heart.

He'd gotten his first email from Maddie that morning. He'd waited to open it, wanting to be alone, and wanting to give himself some time to prepare for what she had to say.

Vivian had written, though. To tell him she loved him,

and that Maddie was doing okay. But also to acknowledge that this was harder than she'd thought it'd be. That Maddie was down and missing home. He thought his aunt probably felt pretty helpless about that. The whole thing was fucked up. And it didn't have to be this way. He could fix it if he could find a little faith within himself. Not a lot. Just a little.

Taking a deep breath, he pulled his phone from his pocket and swiped it open to his email. Staring at Maddie's message, he tapped on it with his thumb.

Hi, Big Brother was the subject line, and his chest immediately tightened.

> *I'm sorry it's taken me so long to write. I guess I was mad, like you said. Leaving Marietta was super hard.*

Tanner looked out over the valley again, his throat aching. He clenched his jaw and blinked up at a hawk circling lazily overhead, wondering how he'd gotten to this place. This place where he'd lost his courage because it had disguised itself as righteousness. Where had he gone so wrong, and how was he just now seeing it for what it was?

He looked back down at his phone, feeling a soft breeze move the hair on his arms.

> *It's taken a while, but I think I get it now. What you said was true. You were only doing what you thought was best for me. And I know you love me a lot. I don't want you to feel bad about sending me to live with Aunt Vivian and Uncle Rob. It's nice here and I'm learning to like it a little. I went boogie boarding yesterday! You would be proud of me.*

I guess what I want to say is that even though I'm not living there with you, you're still a good brother to me. Even from far away. You'll make a great dad someday, too. I know you tried your best after Mom died and I'll always remember that.

I love you, Tanner.

Your sister, Mads

P.S. Can you feed Charlotte a piece of cheese for me? I know you don't like to give her people food, but I've been sneaking it to her and she loves it soooo much. That's why she always wants to be on my lap when we watch movies. Ha ha.

Sometime over the last few minutes, Tanner's vision had begun to blur. Slowly, he put his phone down. The faith that he'd been looking for had been right there, all along. It was the faith Maddie had in him.

And all of a sudden, he saw it. The answer was as clear as the deep blue sky above, as simple as the cry of the hawk in the distance. If he could send her away, and she could love him through that, what's the worse he could do by raising her? He'd make mistakes. Hell, he'd probably screw up left and right. But if he was lucky, he wouldn't have to embark on this alone.

Chapter Twenty-Three

FRANCIE SAT IN front of the movie theater on a little bench overlooking Main Street. With her belly in knots, she watched the people walking past.

The evening was chilly enough that she'd needed to grab a sweater before leaving her house, but she still wore shorts from earlier in the day. Goose bumps marched up and down her legs, but she was too preoccupied with thoughts of Tanner to notice much.

She hadn't seen him in so long, since he'd left for Helena, that when he'd called that afternoon to tell her he was back, she'd been overcome with a strange bundle of nerves.

Meet me in front of the movies at seven? he'd asked. *I need to give you something.*

All afternoon she'd been obsessing over why he didn't just come by her house. But Main Street was neutral territory, right? No chance he'd give in and carry her off to bed, if that's what he was worried about. It'd be a perfect place to tell her he just wanted to be friends from here on out. That he hadn't been blowing smoke before—he really wasn't up for a relationship, and the past few weeks away had solidified that.

She knew he still had a set of keys to her back gate and patio, and that's what he might be wanting to give her.

One of her neighbor's kids walked by with his friends, and he smiled and waved. "Hi, Miss Tate!"

She smiled back. "Hi, Trent." He'd grown over the summer. His hair was longer, shaggier. Only a few more years, and he'd be in middle school. Her heart squeezed. It happened so fast. Too fast.

She thought of Maddie then. She'd texted the day before yesterday and had sounded more upbeat than she had since landing in Honolulu. She'd finally emailed Tanner, and Francie could tell some of the weight she'd been carrying around was beginning to ease a little. She'd told him what she'd needed to—that she understood why he felt like he had to give her up. It had made Francie tear up, but she was proud of her. It was a moment where the little girl in her was meeting the young woman. Maddie still longed for Marietta and her brother, but she forgave him and was ready to move on with her chin up.

The scent of warm popcorn wafted out of the theater, and Francie's stomach growled. She was surprised it was capable of growling, for how tangled up it was. Never in her life had she cared this much about a man. She loved him so much it hurt. But she realized at that moment that it didn't matter how much she loved him. If he didn't love her back, this would be the end of the road. She'd move on. She'd keep her chin up, too. And she'd eventually try and forget about Tanner Harlow and this summer that had burned itself into her heart like the hottest, brightest sun.

And then she looked up and there he was. Walking toward her like he was the only man in town. And he was. The only one who mattered, anyway. He wore a worn pair of jeans and a leather belt that rode low on his hips. He had on a nondescript gray T-shirt that stretched over his broad chest and shoulders just enough to reveal the muscles underneath. It was tucked in only halfway. Like he didn't care if it stayed on or came off. It was all the same to him.

Every female cell in her body tensed at the sight.

When he saw her, he smiled. It was slow at first. Just a tilting of the lips, a teasing of the mouth. And for a second, for one heart bursting second, she didn't think she could take it anymore. The vision of him walking toward her with the evening sun at his back. His silhouette like some kind of Wild West cowboy, coming to take what he wanted. And discard the rest. And then he'd be gone like the leaves from the maples in the fall. So beautiful, the memory so precious.

He slowed as he neared, and she stood, looking up at him.

They regarded each other in silence for a long minute, the people walking by, the cars passing on the street, all lost to Francie.

"My God," he said, his voice low. "You're a sight for sore eyes."

Her hands trembled at that, and she crossed her arms over her chest just to have something to do with them. She smiled because she couldn't help it. Because he made her happy.

"Ditto," she said.

"I've missed you, Francie."

She didn't answer. Just stood there waiting. Waiting for whatever he was going to say and hoping it wouldn't leave her curled up in a little ball.

He looked down at the sidewalk and kicked at a pebble with the toe of his boot. He was unguarded right then. She could see it in the expression on his handsome face, the set of his dark jaw. The angle of his shoulders and his stance. It made her love him even more, if that was possible. Her heart thumped painfully inside her chest.

"I've always loved you," he said quietly. "Even back then. I actually thought about telling you, but I knew if I ever tried, the words wouldn't come out right. They'd get stuck like everything else, and I'd screw it up."

She felt herself tremble. She imagined him telling her he loved her at fifteen. She was glad he didn't. She was glad he hadn't handed that gift to the girl she'd been back then. That girl wouldn't have known what to do with it.

His gaze shifted to hers. And there it settled, like moonlight. Illuminating everything. Illuminating her from the inside, out.

"I'm tired of being afraid," he said. "I'm tired of being scared of fucking up. Letting Maddie go was a mistake. Not letting you in was another one. But it's not too late to fix it."

He stepped closer, and she could see the individual points of stubble peppering his jaw. It was so bold and sexy. Like his eyes and his hair. Like Tanner himself.

He reached for her hand and pulled her close. She went willingly, not wanting to cry, but feeling so much joy well inside her chest, that it was going to be a miracle if she didn't. He was warm and solid. Gentle and strong.

"I love you, Francie," he said. "I love everything about you. I'm sorry it's taken so many years to say it."

Tipping her head back, she smiled her happiest smile. It wasn't her homecoming smile, the one that had made her so popular growing up. It was the one she saved for the moments she felt the safest. The one she gave to the people she loved the most.

"Honestly, it was worth the wait," she said.

He reached up, brushing the backs of his knuckles along her cheekbone. She was vaguely aware of people walking past, smiling at them. She guessed they must look in love. Maybe she was glowing. She felt like she was glowing.

"But one question," she said.

"What's that?"

"What did you want to give me?"

He grinned. Reaching into his back pocket, he pulled out an envelope and handed it to her.

"What…"

"It's a two-way ticket to Honolulu," he said. "Want to come with me to get my little sister back?"

The tears that had been threatening, finally spilled over her cheeks. She felt their warm tracks all the way to her chin. People were staring now, but she didn't care. She hadn't cried enough happy tears in her life, and she was finding that they were now her favorite kind.

He took her face in his hands and brushed the wetness away with his thumbs. "Is that a yes?"

She laughed and nodded. "Yes, Tanner," she said. "That's a yes."

Chapter Twenty-Four

T HE UBER DRIVER was a friendly guy in his mid-fifties. Balding, wearing a bright orange Hawaiian shirt and flip-flops, which Tanner had just learned were referred to as slippers in Hawaii.

His name was Jeff, but everyone called him Ham. They didn't ask why. He'd moved to Oahu twenty years ago from Nebraska and hadn't looked back since. Tanner had liked him instantly and leaned back now to look out the window while holding Francie's hand.

The city slipped busily past their windows. It was a concrete jungle that boasted mountains in the distance that were so green, they were almost neon. The teal waters of the Pacific lapped up onto wide, white beaches, where skyscrapers towered close by.

It was a cloudy day—misty, but still warm. They were headed to Manoa, the quaint, upscale suburb where his aunt and uncle lived.

Tanner had called Vivian two days ago, telling her they were coming, and why. She'd been dismissive at first, saying things were already settled. But after almost half an hour of argument, she'd told him they'd talk when he got there.

He'd asked her to keep it a secret from Maddie, who loved surprises, and he heard Vivian's voice soften then. *She'll be beside herself,* she'd said.

They finally turned onto Vivian and Rob's street, which hadn't changed much since Tanner had been there in elementary school. He rolled down the window and breathed in the heavy air, which smelled like plumerias.

Francie squeezed his hand and he turned to her. She was beautiful—fresh faced, with her hair pulled into a high ponytail. There were two bright spots of color on her cheeks, and he knew she could hardly wait to see Maddie. But like him, she realized he might be in for a fight. There was just no way of knowing until Vivian opened the door.

He'd talked to both Luke and Judd last night. They were both set to move back to Marietta. Judd was in the process of getting his hub changed to Bozeman and would sublease his apartment in Indianapolis. Luke would be done with his tour in December and would hopefully be home in time for Christmas. Among the three of them, Maddie would have a close, stable family unit who'd do anything for her. If that wasn't a sticking point for Vivian, he didn't know what would be.

Ham glanced over his shoulder. "Five hundred and forty? That the address?"

"That's it," Tanner said, watching the houses pass by one by one.

"Here we are. Looks like that beige one with the white trim." Ham pulled over to the curb. "Should I wait?"

Tanner pulled out his wallet and handed him a twenty.

"No, man. That's okay. Keep the change."

"Thanks, sir. You folks have a nice visit, okay?"

"Next time you're in Montana, look us up," Francie said.

"Will do."

The air outside the car was humid. A big, beautiful co-
conut tree in the yard shivered in the breeze, and as they
walked up to the deck, a gecko scurried underneath their
feet. Francie jumped, covering her mouth before she
screamed.

He laughed, pulling her close. "Welcome to Hawaii."

She held his hand as they walked up the steps and came
to a stop at the door.

"You ready?" she asked.

"Ready as I'll ever be." He took a deep breath and rang
the doorbell.

After a few seconds, Vivian opened it wearing a genuine
smile.

She wrapped Tanner in a perfumey hug, then pulled
away to look up at him. "Handsome as ever."

"Hi, Aunt Viv."

She turned to Francie and hugged her, too.

"It's good to see you again, Mrs. Craig," Francie said.

"Vivian, please." Her smiled faded as she took them both
in. "Rob's at work. We'll see him at dinner. Maddie's riding
her bike but should be back any minute. I haven't said
anything."

Tanner nodded. "Thanks for that. She's a sucker for surprises."

Vivian wrung her hands together. "She's a sucker for a

lot of things. Her brother, for one."

"Vivian…" Tanner began.

"I know what you're going to say. We've been over it and over it, and I still think this is the best place for her." She paused, staring into her yard where every different kind of flower imaginable bloomed. "But I underestimated how much she'd miss you. How much she loves Montana. I was wrong to brush that aside, and I'm sorry."

"I miss her, too," he said.

"We've done everything we can think of to make her feel at home here. Taken her to the beach and the park. Introduced her to neighbor kids and set up movie dates. But she's barely wanted to come out of her room. She's been so withdrawn. It's heartbreaking, really."

Tanner couldn't stand the thought of Maddie sad. He should never have sent her away. He should've kept her close and told her she'd have a home with him for as long as she wanted one. He should've been the father she never had. But one thing he'd learned these last few weeks, was that regret got you nowhere. He'd made a mistake. And now it was time to make it right.

"I know it's hard," he said. "Figuring out the right thing always is. But she'll have a good home with us, Aunt Vivian. It's where she belongs."

She opened her mouth to reply but stopped and looked over his shoulder.

He and Francie turned to see Maddie standing at the end of the stone pathway. She was holding her bike up by the handlebars. Her helmet, which looked too big, drooped toward one eye as she stared at them in utter disbelief.

"Tanner?"

He broke into a grin, and the heaviness that he'd grown so used to since she'd left lifted from his shoulders.

She dropped her bike and ran to him. He'd barely gotten down the steps before she launched herself into his arms. Catching her, he swung her around in a full circle, her gangly legs flying off to the side. Her hair was damp from the mist, but her skin was warm and soft. Like a baby's. He remembered helping her learn how to ride a bike. He remembered cleaning up her knees after she'd fallen and telling her it was going to be all right. He was there. He'd always be there.

He stopped spinning her, and came to a stop on the walkway, holding her close as she cried against his chest. She weighed barely anything at all.

After a minute, after she'd calmed some, he set her back down and held her by the shoulders. "Hey, you."

"Tanner." Her glasses were knocked crooked and she reached up to straighten them. "And Francie, you too?"

"I wouldn't miss it for the world, honey," Francie said.

Tanner glanced back at the two women standing on the porch. Vivian sniffed and wiped her nose with a Kleenex. Smiling, Francie put an arm around her. It was a moment he knew he'd always remember.

Maddie reached for his hand and held it tight, as if she were afraid he'd yank it back again. "I've missed you so much."

"Hey," he said. "I've got something for you."

"What?"

He pulled a purple striped sock from his pocket and handed it over.

"My other sock! These are my favorite! Where'd you find it?"

"In Charlotte's bed."

Maddie grinned.

"I think she stole it on purpose," he said. "She's been sleeping with it since you left, like a blankie."

"*Charlotte*. Did you feed her some cheese? Please say you fed her some cheese."

He rolled his eyes. "Yes, I've been feeding her cheese, and now she expects to sit at the dinner table like a person."

She giggled, and the sound was like a bell. He'd missed that laugh. He hadn't realized how quiet his house had been without it.

She looked from him, to Francie, to Vivian, and back again, her smile fading. "What's going on, anyway?"

This was it. The moment he'd come here for. Vivian made her way down the steps, her heels clicking hollowly on the wood panels. Francie followed, ready to give him her support. Ready to fight alongside him if necessary. He loved her so much right then, because other than his brothers, he'd never had anyone stand up with him before. She was tender, fierce, lovely. The entire package. And she was his.

He turned to his aunt, a formidable woman in her pressed slacks and immaculate blouse. She used to intimidate him when he was little. But he'd also looked up to her, respected her because she was someone who knew what she wanted and didn't stop until she got it. She'd be a tough adversary. But that was the thing—he didn't want her to be an adversary. He wanted her to be family. He wanted them all to be family.

Steeling himself, he opened his mouth to tell Maddie he'd come to take her back, but Vivian spoke first.

"Do you like it here, sweetheart?"

Maddie frowned and looked down at her feet. "I do."

"But you like it better in Marietta, don't you?"

"Yes."

"Tanner tells me he wants to raise you," Vivian said. "I can see how much he loves you. Would you like to go back with him and Francie?"

Maddie broke into a ridiculous, toothy smile.

Francie walked up beside Tanner and hooked her arm in his. He covered her hand with his own as he watched his aunt.

Vivian smiled slowly, her eyes bright. "My sister may not have been perfect. But she managed to have four beautiful children who love each other very much. Your uncle and I don't want to come between you. We only want what's best. It's clear now this is it." She looked at Tanner then and reached up to touch his face. "I misjudged you. You're going to make a wonderful father."

Maddie wrapped her arms around his waist, and he could feel her heart beating, fast like a bird's. He felt the sun's warmth as it broke through the clouds, and damn if there wasn't a rainbow forming right behind Vivian's house.

They all turned and looked at the same time. Maybe it was his mom. He'd never been one to believe in signs or fate, but today, he thought he might. He knew he could thank Francie for that, standing quietly beside him. And Maddie's sweet smile. And the confident look in his aunt's eyes.

Today was the first day of the rest of his life.

And it was a good one.

Epilogue

F RANCIE STOOD WITH Tanner's arm firmly around her
waist. He was holding her strongly, fiercely. As if she
were his. And she guessed she was, officially.

They watched from Francie's porch as Maddie and Colton made their way down the sidewalk, the crispy autumn
leaves skipping haphazardly across Bramble Lane. It was early
yet, but there were already some ghosts and goblins making
their way from house to house for candy bars and the
occasional dreaded toothbrush. The air was chilly and
smelled of wood smoke. Francie breathed it in, feeling utterly
blissful in the moment.

Tanner looked down at her, his face a study in big brother worry. "You think they'll be okay?"

She smiled. "I think they'll be more than okay. Maddie's
entire basketball team will be there. Plus about four chaper-
ones. They'll have a blast. It's only a few blocks to the
movies, and we're picking them up after so they won't even
have to walk in the dark, remember?"

"But *The Lost Boys?* Too freaky?"

She leaned into his side. "It's vintage Jason Patrick. Trust
me, she'll thank you later."

His eyes were a dark chocolate brown in the fading evening light. The beginnings of a beard graced his jaw and neck, making him look rugged and unattainable. Then she remembered she'd attained him. Every tall, dark, handsome bit of him. He was hers, and she was his.

His lips curved slowly. "How would I do this without you?"

"You'd do just fine. You're learning. We both are."

They looked up when Maddie stopped and waved from down the dusky street. "Love you!" she yelled.

Francie's heart swelled. There'd be a time when she'd be too embarrassed for this kind of thing. But she wasn't now, and the fact that she was still very much a little girl, despite how much taller she'd gotten over the summer, made Francie want to cry.

Tanner waved back as they watched the kids turn the corner and disappear out of sight.

Then, squeezing her waist, he nudged her toward the door. "I got two extra bags of candy, but it looks like we're gonna be inundated. Pizza should be here any minute, though. Ready for the movie?"

"I'm ready for some light necking. Maybe more."

"Oh, yeah?"

She laughed as he leaned down to nuzzle behind her ear. His beard tickled the sensitive skin there and gave her chills. Yeah, okay. So maybe she hadn't been kidding about the necking part.

They headed inside with Charlotte at their heels, Tanner flipping on the porch light as they went. But before they could close the door, the soft purr of a car pulling up to the curb stopped them.

Francie turned to see her mother getting out of her sleek, midnight-blue Audi. She held something wrapped in foil, as she walked around the car and stepped onto the curb in her trendy calf-length boots.

"Mom?" Her stomach tightened. She'd found peace with a lot of things lately, her relationship with her mother being one of them. It would probably always be complicated. But the days of Loretta controlling Francie's every move through her upbringing and resulting guilt were over. They'd negotiated an unsteady truce a few weeks ago, but Loretta hadn't met Tanner yet. Francie had been protective of their newborn relationship, and even though she was so proud of him it hurt, she hadn't wanted to subject him to her mother's judgements just yet.

She felt the gentle weight of Tanner's hand at the small of her back. He knew exactly how she felt. Ironically, he usually sided with Loretta. *Give her another chance. You could both use a fresh start...* All families deserve that, right? Maybe that was his own peacefulness showing through. He'd finally forgiven his mother for everything she'd done and not done when he'd been a kid, and the result was that he was a much happier man. A man who was able to let go of the past and move toward the future.

She knew she could learn a thing or two from him.

Loretta smiled, holding up the tinfoil mystery package. "I brought caramel-covered apples. Your favorite, remember?"

Despite her knotted belly, Francie smiled back, feeling a

rush of affection for the only mother she'd ever known. Flawed or not, she was her mom.

"Of course, I remember. Thanks, Mom."

Loretta walked up the steps, her heels clicking on the wood, as Charlotte came trotting out to meet her. Tanner lunged forward and grabbed her collar before she could thrust her nose in Loretta's crotch.

Francie gave her a hug and took the apples. Drawing a deep breath, she glanced over at Tanner. This was it. No more pretending, no more protecting. This was her life. And it wasn't perfect. It was messy and layered, and she loved it with all her heart.

"Mom, I'd like you to meet—"

"Tanner." Loretta's glossy pink lips stretched into a smile. Not a beauty-queen smile. A real smile. Something coveted, because Francie recognized it for what it was. Genuine.

"I've heard a lot about you," she continued.

Tanner leaned down and gave her a hug. His hugs were one of his newest and best qualities. They had the ability to melt even the frostiest of hearts. Although, her mom didn't look frosty right then. Far from it.

Loretta laughed, obviously expecting a hand shake, or something just as formal.

"It's nice to meet you, Mrs. Tate," Tanner said, pulling away.

"Loretta, please."

"Loretta."

She glanced over at Francie and her eyes were a little sad

then. Something brief passed over them—maybe regret for time lost, or the realization they hadn't fully understood each other until just recently. Francie could only guess. But that's how *she* felt right then. And her chest warmed.

"I'm sorry it's taken me so long to come by, Tanner," Loretta said, looking back at him.

"No worries. We've all been busy."

"That's not it." Her tone wasn't clipped, but there was an assertiveness there that Francie hadn't heard before. It was a stark contrast to the honeyed voice that always told her to put her shoulders back and smile. Smile no matter what.

"If I've learned anything from my daughter these past few weeks," she continued, "it's that we all need to say what we feel more often. Even if it's not the most comfortable thing."

Francie put her hand on her mom's arm.

Loretta smiled, but didn't take her gaze off Tanner's. "So I'm going to be honest and say that when I found out how she felt about you I was skeptical. I'm not proud of that, but I was. For reasons I can't even explain to you right now. At least not in any way that makes sense."

Tanner watched her steadily, his eyes kind. "You don't know me. Maybe you had reasons to be skeptical."

"I know enough. I know that you're a hard worker. I know that you're choosing to raise your little sister. I know that you're an important member of this community, and that my daughter loves you. That's really all I need to know."

Francie swallowed the sizeable lump in her throat and looked up at Tanner. He was one of the toughest people she'd ever met. But there was something in his expression that said even after how far he'd come, maybe he needed to hear that right then. Maybe he'd needed to hear it all along. Not just the man, but the boy from so long ago.

She pictured him reading from *The Catcher in the Rye*, with his dark mop of hair falling over one eye, and his voice that kept stumbling. And she knew she'd started falling in love with him that very moment. On that chilly fall day that wasn't so different from the evening they were standing in now.

Tanner pushed the door open farther and stepped aside, his house, his heart, finally an open book. "We've got pizza coming," he said. "Why don't you stay awhile?"

The End

The Harlow Brother Series

Book 1: *Tanner's Promise*

Book 2: *Luke's Gift*

Book 3: *Coming soon*

Available now at your favorite online retailer!

More books by Kaylie Newell

Christmas at the Graff
2018 RITA® nominated for Contemporary Romance: Short

Falling for the Ranger

Available now at your favorite online retailer!

About the Author

For Kaylie Newell, storytelling is in the blood. Growing up the daughter of two gifted writers, she knew eventually she'd want to follow in their footsteps. While she's written short stories her whole life, it wasn't until after her kids were born that she decided to shoot for the moon and write her first romance novel. She hasn't looked back since!

Kaylie lives in Southern Oregon with her husband, two little girls, two indifferent cats and a mutt named Pedro.

Visit Kaylie at KaylieNewell.com

Thank you for reading

Tanner's Promise

If you enjoyed this book, you can find more from all our great authors at TulePublishing.com, or from your favorite online retailer.

TULE
PUBLISHING

48321531R00135

Made in the USA
Middletown, DE
14 June 2019